NEW YEAR'S PROMISE

TALES OF AMISH SISTERS SERIES, BOOK 2

GRACE LEWIS

COPYRIGHT © 2024 BY GRACE LEWIS

BOOK DESCRIPTION

Ringing in a new year brings hope, renewal, and the promise of fresh starts. But for two Amish sisters carrying tender scars, embracing the future requires letting go of the past.

Still mourning her husband's passing, young widow Beth Fisher faces the New Year alone for the second time. Managing her grief and new motherhood duties strains her resilience to its limits. The compassion of widower Samuel seems like more than she can accept right now, despite her heart longing for partnership.

Beth's sister Naomi finally married her sweetheart Isaac, only to have their joy marred by lingering gossip about her reputation. As New

Year's nears, Isaac's former love returning in the community ignites Naomi's old insecurities. She struggles to leave the past behind and build faith in their future together.

Against a backdrop of forbidden desires, village rumors, and spiritual questioning, two vulnerable sisters cross an emotional threshold to being the new year with hope renewed and hearts made whole. Will family bonds and their community's faith buoy them through the darkness?

Join the Fisher sisters on a poignant journey through adversity toward the redemptive power of forgiveness and new beginnings this New Year's season.

Notes: Each book in the series is a stand-alone read, but to make the most of the series you should consider reading them in order. All Grace Lewis's books are clean and wholesome Amish romance.

FOREWORD

This book is dedicated to you, the reader.

Thank you for taking a chance on me, and for joining me on this journey.

Do you want to keep up to date with all of my latest releases, and **start reading *Rumspringa's Promise*, *Secret Love* and *River Blessings*, exclusive spinoffs from the *Seasons of Love*, *Amish Hearts* and the *Amish Sisters series*, for free?**

Join my readers' group (copy and paste this link into your browser: *bit.ly/Grace-FreeBook*). Details can be found at the end of the book.

PROLOGUE

Sitting by the window, Naomi pushed the needle through the latest square for her quilt for baby Eli, her nephew. She had hesitated to come to the quilting circle. Married to Isaac for a few months, Naomi still didn't feel totally accepted by the rest of the community. She had joined this quilting circle to forge more friendships. She had planned to go there with her sister Beth, but she had to look after Eli this afternoon and wanted to be alone in the *haus* with him.

As luck would have it, the club was meeting at the home of Sarah King, one of her friends. Most people were in their own headspace, working on a quilt. However, there were still whisperings of gossip passing around the room. Having been the topic of gossip herself before, Naomi did her best to focus on the quilt and ignore them. Not wanting to get involved, she got up and went to the kitchen, pretending to pour herself a glass of water.

As she walked back into the room, approaching the door, she heard one of the women whispering her name. Despite herself, her heartbeat had quickened, and she stopped before entering the room to listen.

"I cannot believe she still thinks she might be fully accepted," one woman whispered nearby. "She did so much wrong on her *rumspringa*. Does she truly believe she could be a full member, whatever the bishop says?"

"I mean, you hear her tales of going back into the city!" Another woman—and keeping in mind they were both older, perhaps in their forties or fifties—continued the hushed conversation. "Who is to say she's not keeping in touch with her friends from her *rumspringa*? I don't care what the bishop says."

Naomi's stomach sunk. She didn't need to listen to all of this. Again. Not today. After months of marriage, she had hoped that people would start appreciating her skills in the bakery instead of looking down on her for faking her repentance.

She still wondered how one could fake repentance.

To put on a brave face, she composed a fake smile, and she returned to her seat. She quickly finished the edge of the square and packed her things.

"Naomi? Are you all right?" Sarah's voice stopped her.

"I'm feeling a little ill. Perhaps I ought to leave before I make anyone else ill," Naomi said softly.

She didn't want Sarah to feel responsible for the gossip going on; it was one of those ill-conceived side effects of getting all the women in the community together.

"At least let me help you to the buggy."

And with that thought, she pulled herself away from the window.

"*Nee, danke,*" Naomi said. "I can get there on my own."

Sarah nodded slowly. Naomi walked out of the home with her quilting supplies. As she got into the buggy, she couldn't help but look at the world around her. With fall slowly approaching winter, there was little left for her to do in preparation for the changing of the seasons. Her *daed* still appreciated her help around his bakery, but today, she was not needed for the simple fact that it hadn't been busy. This was the slowest time of year. It would pick up again in a month.

That gave her a month to get her *haus* in order before the holidays came around. Once the holidays arrived, she would be dealing with as many *Englischers* as she could handle, and then some. For some reason, the Christmas sweets always brought them in droves.

She shook her head.

"One day at a time, Naomi. One day at a time. That's how you got here. That's how you'll get anywhere in life," she whispered as she felt the rumblings of anxiety in her stomach. " Since Isaac is busy, I think it's time I got decluttering some of the other areas in the *haus*."

As she headed into the kitchen to start on the dishes from breakfast, she wasn't sure of her many feelings.

Since marrying Isaac, she had learned that thinking hard about the future would only end in more worry. Especially if she allowed the gossip to dictate what she thought about. However, she knew that that was not what she needed to do today.

"So, what if they think I haven't changed enough?" Naomi continued to muse to herself as she began to fill the sink to wash the dishes. "There is nothing about being Amish that means I have to listen to their rumors. At least that much, I learned on my *rumspringa*. If nothing else, perhaps that's the best lesson I learned while I was away."

She took in a deep breath, and then plunged her hands into the water as she started to scrub at the dishes that had been sitting there for about thirty minutes. Half of her issue, it seemed at times, was that she got so easily lost in thought that she forgot that she could talk to Isaac about any thought bothering her.

After a good talk the night before about the troubling rumors she was hearing, they had decided that it wasn't worth paying attention to them. Despite the welling pit in her stomach, Naomi was determined to keep that spirit this year.

As she washed the dishes, she hummed one of her favorite hymns to distract herself. Some spring cleaning would do not only her soul some good, but also her home. As newlyweds, they had received numerous gifts. However, quite a few had not been used because some of her *Englischer* friends had gotten them typical gifts for a city wedding.

What were they supposed to do with a stand mixer when they had no electricity?

Naomi had half a mind to send all the new goods gifted from her *Englischer* friends into town and donate them because someone else could get some good use out of them. She'd have to find someone to go with her, then, because she didn't like to go alone. That single act of going by herself would also stir up far more gossip than was worth it.

∼

BETH FISHER HELD HER *SOHN*, Eli, in her arms. He was about eight months old now. Every time she thought he couldn't get cuter, he proved her wrong. However, there was more to her life right now than little Eli. She wished it wasn't the case, for her own sake.

Living with her parents while taking care of a newborn had proven to be one of the most difficult things she had ever done.

As a single *mamm* in the Amish community, she was finding that she faced certain stigmas far more than even Naomi had faced scrutiny after returning from her *rumspringa*. She wasn't entirely sure how to feel about it. Beth wanted to do the best she could for her *sohn*, but there was only so much she could do alone. Especially when the community saw no qualms with telling her so.

Her *mamm* watched Eli while Beth worked in their bakery, which helped her find a way to be productive without having to worry about Eli, but even this got her criticized for not caring enough about Eli to stay home with him all day, everyday. He'd be crawling within a couple of months, if not sooner. As much as she wanted to be there for that, she knew that she also needed to find support outside her own *familye*.

She shook those thoughts away. Today, she and her *mamm* were sitting in the living room. Eli sat on the floor, surrounded by a blanket and pillows. He had a small wooden rocking horse to play with and a rattle made by the carpenter in the community. If that wasn't enough stimulation for now, Beth wasn't sure what would be.

"How are you feeling today, Beth?" Clara asked.

Beth turned to face her *mamm*. As much as she appreciated all she was doing for her, there were days that her *mamm* pressed too hard. She hadn't yet today, but Beth knew that this conversation was going to go down roads she wasn't ready to traverse yet if she wasn't careful.

"I wish I had more people who understood what I'm going through," Beth admitted. "There's so much to think about as a single *mamm*. And I don't think there's a widow in the community who gained such a status while pregnant like I did."

She hefted a sigh as she moved from her seat on the couch to sit on the floor beside Eli.

"Eli's a *wunderbar* part of my life, *Mamm*, but… why do I always feel so exhausted?"

"If I may give advice without you feeling that it's out of my wheelhouse?" Her *mamm* raised an eyebrow. "Beth, you tend to get a little touchy with me when I offer advice…"

"What is it?" Beth asked in return.

"I think you're finding it so hard to be a single *mamm* because parenthood is not designed for one person to bear alone," Clara replied. "While you have some help in the form of me and your *dued,* and through Naomi and Isaac, there's meant to be more help at your home than there is from *familye*."

"Are you suggesting what I think you're suggesting?" Beth gave her *mamm* a look.

She hardly had time to take care of herself

some days as she was making sure that Eli's needs were all met. If she were to try to court, she didn't think it'd go very well because she didn't want to put more of Eli's care on her parents or on her *schweschder*.

Eli was her *kind*. Beth should be the one seeing to all the hard parts, in her opinion, not her *familye*.

"I'm not suggesting anything," Clara clarified. "I'm simply saying that maybe you need to give some thought as to whether it would be worth courting *menner* while raising a *kind*. It is possible. I'm not sure how, but where there's a prayer, there's a way."

Beth pressed her lips together slowly.

She'd given this option some serious consideration in months past. She always came to the same conclusion. With the way her life was right now, she just didn't have the emotional wherewithal to give a *mann* the proper consideration. She wanted to raise Eli right, with a *daed* that he could look up to.

But how did she get that for him without feeling like she was abandoning him now to do so?

"You don't have to say or do anything with it right now," Clara continued. "I just think you need to know that you're not meant to be raising a *kind* alone. No woman is."

Beth nodded slowly.

"I'll take your advice into consideration, I suppose," she said. "But, *Mamm,* I have little hope that I will be able to do that and take care of Eli all at once. It's a lot to ask."

CHAPTER 1

After cleaning the breakfast dishes, Naomi decided that it was time to go through the boxes in the upstairs closet. She was pretty sure that they had nothing more to hide in there. Besides, keeping boxes packed up made her feel as though they hadn't officially finished the move. Or that this *haus* didn't officially belong to them.

All the boxes needed to get cleaned out, and their contents put away. This *haus* belonged to them. It was time to make it feel that way.

One of the first boxes she opened contained mementos of her *rumspringa*. They weren't sentimental, and all she cared to keep was a rock she had found while on a walk. It looked like a heart – weathered into that shape by the creek in which she had found it. The find had been most interesting.

As Naomi held it in her hands again, she remembered how she felt finding it in the water. Her pocket had been soaked for the rest of the walk, but she beamed when she showed everyone else what she had found. She remembered sharing a scripture about love and the way it shaped the world, but she couldn't remember the exact scripture anymore.

Perhaps that was for the best, but she wished she could remember. That scripture would probably come in handy when she struggled to remember how to love herself.

She set it on her bedside table to remind her that love could come in the most peculiar ways. She'd shared stories about this rock with Isaac. Being able to share it with him tonight, letting him see what she had seen, sounded like a perfect way to end a long, hard day of cleaning.

She returned to the box in the closet and decided to pull the box out of the closet. There was no point in keeping it in there if she was eventually going to collapse it.

She realized it was heavier than she expected as she set it down on the bed with a sigh. Since this box held old mementos of favorite memories, and they had wanted to fill their home with happiness, this would be the box to start them off on the right foot.

"What in the world is in this box that's making it so heavy?"

She opened the flaps and started to unpack the box a little more thoroughly, putting the contents onto the bed. While it was mostly small items such as letters from friends, it wasn't until she found a small photo box that the weight issue made sense. As she lifted it out of the box, she almost grunted with the effort.

She did not remember carrying such a heavy item up to their bedroom. Then again, perhaps Isaac had carried it to save her the exertion. She had been quite tired on the day they moved in.

Instead of putting the photo box on the bed, she took it to the bedside table. This deserved a proper look.

What had Isaac put in here? It had to have been his since she didn't recognize it, and he had started this box. She finished packing it after directing the placement of the kitchen items from her *Englischer* friends.

When she opened the box, she found more letters.

"That's odd. If it's only letters, why keep them

here? To keep them from getting wrinkled?" She pursed her lips.

It wasn't until she saw who had written them that she started to wonder why these had been kept. Isaac had courted in his past, just like she had. However, she hadn't kept anything given to her or written to her during that time. These letters were written to Isaac by the woman he had courted by the name of Hannah.

Naomi may not have written Isaac letters, but he hadn't kept anything that she had given him. Perhaps because her offerings had been in the way of food and had been finished before they had to be thrown away. It still didn't stop the welling jealousy, but she did manage to stop herself from crushing the letter in her hand. Instead, she simply put it back in the box and put it on Isaac's bedside table.

Even if he didn't think that it was worth throwing away, he should have warned her that he kept them. This was an unexpected surprise that she was not enjoying.

She glanced out the window. The sun was beginning to set, which meant Isaac would be home soon enough. Perhaps it was time to talk to him about the expectations now that they were married. How long would he have left these letters in their closet, unknown to her?

She walked into the living room, where she set about sweeping the dirt off the floor which was unacceptable to Naomi in her cleaning mood.

Isaac got home only a few minutes later, tapping his boots at the door to prevent tracking in more dirt. She appreciated that. At least he was aware that she had been cleaning unless he knew that the treads of his shoes were particularly dirty today and needed a good cleaning off before entering the house.

"I'm home!" He smiled as he walked inside.

Naomi caught the smile because she was looking at him.

"Is… is something wrong?" The smile quickly faded when he saw her face, making her think that her expression might be a lot sourer than she intended.

"Isaac, I found letters in the closet addressed to you from Hannah," she said.

If she was going to ask him about it, she figured that it was best to be upfront and just ask him about it rather than dance around the question. Besides, Isaac appreciated her straightforwardness. When she remembered to be so, at least. Sometimes, he had to ask her multiple times what was wrong.

"Oh. Those letters," he said, although he didn't seem entirely too concerned about how she was feeling about them. "I thought I warned you. I'm not sure what I want to do with them. They are indeed love letters if that's your next question."

"What was the relationship like for you to keep the love letters years after you've moved on, and have married another woman?" Naomi asked.

As much as she didn't like what she felt, she knew that it wouldn't go away until she was satisfied that he had told her everything about the relationship.

He sighed, instead of offering an explanation immediately. She wasn't sure what that meant, but she continued to wait for an answer. At this point, he needed to share everything that he had been hiding about the relationship with Hannah because she didn't want to come to a wrong conclusion.

"We had a youthful romance," Isaac finally said. "It ended when she left me. Rather painfully, might I add. I suppose I've not dealt with the letters because I don't like the feelings they dredge up. I don't remember which box I put them in.

What were you doing that you found them?" He raised an eyebrow.

She supposed that was a fair question.

"I was unpacking boxes in the closet," she replied softly. "Isaac... I didn't think I'd come across love letters from a woman you had previously courted while I was unpacking for our marital home."

"You don't need to worry about Hannah," he said. "She left the community for another Amish community, and I believe she has no intentions of returning. I've not had communication with her since she left me. It was that bad a heartbreak."

She nodded slowly.

That helped her nerves, but she was still unhappy about the fact that he had kept these letters. Why would he dare to keep them when he knew that he was getting married?

"Then, I suggest you find a place to put them where I won't run into them again," Naomi finally said. "I didn't appreciate that, Isaac. Finding those letters wasn't a pleasant feeling. I'd rather not have to feel that way again if we can help it."

Isaac pursed his lips, but she walked into the kitchen to start on dinner before he could ask for any clarification. He didn't need to know what she had felt when she found those letters.

Simply that she didn't like the feelings that it had stirred up in her and she didn't think it was fair on either of them for her to feel like that. Especially with the rumors about her going around. With their speculations that she had asked for the items from her *Englischer* friends so that she was ready to leave at a moment's notice – since someone had gifted her luggage, as a rite of passage gift they had said – she didn't need to have anyone else aware of her feelings of jealousy.

She took a moment in the kitchen to take a deep breath. There was no need to be this angry as she made dinner. Once her hands stopped shaking, she walked back to the counter where she had been preparing. As she cut the chicken for soup, making sure to remove all the bones, she tried to calm down.

If Isaac said he was going to take care of the letters, then she had to respect that they would get taken care of. Besides, they were all yellowing. It appeared that he had at least been telling the truth when he said that he hadn't contacted her since they had ended their relationship.

CHAPTER 2

As Christmas inched ever closer, Beth found the exhilarating season completely exhausting. After her complicated birth last Christmas, she was surprised that she was able to do anything even half-speed to keep up with her *familye*. Her parents had always loved this time of year. Her memories were full of the best dinners being on Christmas Day, and of having some of the best times of her life because it was a day purely for *familye* and for celebration. But it demanded earlier preparations with a *boppli* in the *haus* this year.

Usually, Beth would have been delighted to be taking care of any preparations that needed to be done in advance. She had made wreaths and gathered pine boughs the November before, which was always relaxing.

However, the birth of her *sohn* caused her to lose the ability to move her legs for a while. Now that she was regaining her mobility, she found that her body wasn't moving as smoothly, as quickly, or as easily as she would have liked it to in the busy holiday season. She could bend at the waist but bending to pick anything off the floor resulted in her having to hunch over to catch her breath afterwards.

Even holding Eli and moving with the extra weight was a struggle. She was determined to manage Eli but she was not yet up to taking on a heavier weight than him. This meant that the gathering of pine boughs for the *haus* and for the bakery would fall to Naomi this year, more than likely. The *familye* hadn't yet decided, but she could see the concern in everyone's faces when she spoke of wishing to gather pine boughs.

In fact, while Beth held Eli as he slowly fell asleep, she stared longingly out the window. With the snow and ice only a few days away at this point, she wondered what she would be able to do to help with the Christmas preparations.

She glanced down at Eli and found that he had finally fallen asleep. She slowly got up from rocking him to sleep on the rocking chair and gently put him in his crib. Thankfully, she didn't have to bend all the way down. Her body could handle that much, at least.

When she left his room, she shut the door as quietly as she could before making her way to the dining room.

As she walked, she remained close to the wall. A few times this month, with the cold and the weather changes, she had found her body less resilient and weaker than it should have been. She could walk just fine, but had to walk slower than she would have liked in the cold.

Upon arriving in the dining room, she was glad to see that she was able to take a moment to rest. She sat down, letting out a soft sigh.

She wondered if part of her issues remaining from the complications stemmed from not having enough help around the *haus* with Eli. She still had to work at the bakery, and that had been hard at first – especially in the summer. She found herself less able to handle the heat. The faintest hint that the room was too warm – not even hot, just too warm – and she would feel sleepy. On more than one occasion, the heat over the summer had led to her passing out and hitting her head.

That probably hadn't helped her mobility issues, now that she thought about it. But what else could she do?

She got up from the chair and started to make herself some lunch, shaking those thoughts away. This winter, she was learning she had a small window of comfortable temperatures. The summer got far too hot for her in the bakery, and the *haus* didn't get quite warm enough in the winter without a fire going in the living room.

"Is my life doomed to be exacerbated by issues I never asked for?" Beth wondered aloud as she made her sandwich.

She was too exhausted to make anything more filling, or more elaborate. However, after she finished eating, she still had a mountain of chores to accomplish. Her parents had only one rule for her if she wasn't at the bakery, and that was that she had to make sure the *haus* stayed in good order. They didn't expect it to be spotless, but reasonably clean.

Even reasonably clean felt like too much to ask of her on some days, depending on how fussy Eli was.

"I wish Jacob were still here…" Beth mused, grabbing a rag to wipe the counters down. "He would have happily told my parents that I was in no condition to do so much after Eli was born."

She took in a deep breath. It was odd how she was trying to get everything taken care of and feeling like she wasn't getting it done.

Draping the rag over the edge of the sink to dry instead of wiping the counters, Beth felt a lump in her throat. Just thinking about her late husband had gotten the memories rolling. While he may have been a *mann* with struggles – struggling with the nature of alcohol, as she had learned this time last year – he had been trying to do better. He'd wanted to be sober for their *boppli*. For her when he was needed the most.

However, they had *gut* memories too. She remembered when he had proposed, mainly. It had been a small gesture, no grand fanfare. On her *rumspringa*, she had seen quite a few proposals that had made her uncomfortable because clearly, the *mann* was looking to get a 'yes' that he may not have otherwise. Proposing in public in front of strangers was not what she had wanted. Nor was it the Amish way of doing these things.

Jacob had done his proposal well. He'd taken her out for a picnic in the orchard that the community maintained. It had been a beautiful fall day, and there were plenty of apples ripe and ready for picking. They'd had fresh apple pie that day.

He had asked for her hand in marriage after eating the pie, while they were walking around the orchard. They'd found a tree that had been struggling to blossom, but that year, it had the largest crop of apples out of all of the trees in the orchard. Still did, if she remembered correctly.

Her cheek was suddenly wet, and Beth was pulled out of the memories. She wiped her cheek, only to realize that there were tears running down her face. Jacob may not have been the ideal husband at times, especially as the alcohol had turned him quite cold to her, but he was hers. He had made his vows to her at the wedding. Not to anyone else.

She leaned against the counter she'd meant to clean, her head in her hands as the tears continued to run. With her parents out of the *haus* and Naomi and Isaac off doing their own thing in their own home, Beth felt that she could finally let out all the tears. She'd been hiding this from her *familye* for almost a year, and she worried that she would never get over Jacob.

Part of her troubles came from all the bittersweet memories that came up when she thought about moving on. Jacob had done his best with what he had access to. That is how she chose to remember him, even though remembering the sting of finding out how he died was part of the bittersweetness of the memories of her life as a married woman.

When the door opened in the living room, Beth took a moment to wipe her face off and turned to grab the rag. It was still damp and she started wiping down the table, ignoring the messy counter for now. Eli was all right in his crib, and since she had left the door open, she'd hear him cry or wake up.

While she was wiping the table down, her parents came into the room.

"Where's Eli?" Clara asked softly.

"He's in his crib," Beth replied, struggling to keep her voice even. "Hopefully, he'll remain asleep for another hour or two. I just put him down for a nap."

Her *mamm* nodded. Her *daed* just put the large bag of flour on the table, careful not to let the flour get wet.

"*Danke* for cleaning up in here while we were gone," Amos said. "I wasn't sure we'd be able to do it if we had to when we got home. It was a lot heavier than I thought it would be, the flour. And I still have to go get more for the bakery."

"Perhaps Naomi or Isaac could help with the flour for the bakery," Beth offered. "I know that I don't have the time to be helping with the supplies, but I hope that at least by keeping the *haus* clean, I'm doing something… productive."

She didn't know why that was the word that came to mind, but it felt right. She wanted to have no time to think about the bittersweet memories around her *familye* because they'd encourage her to go out and make new ones with someone else.

And Beth wasn't quite sure how she'd manage that with all the struggles she was already facing, trying to care for Eli with their help.

"That's actually a *gut* idea. I don't know why I didn't think of that. I'll be back," Amos said. "Give Eli a hug for me when he wakes up."

With that, her *daed* left the house again.

CHAPTER 3

As snow fell that December, Naomi returned to work at her *daed's* bakery. Clara was at home, looking after Eli. This left Naomi, Beth, and Amos in the bakery to fill the orders. Naomi was quite happy to see that Beth was at least feeling up to the hustle and bustle of the busy season. She'd been struggling over the summer when the orders weren't quite as many and heavy. It meant that whatever had happened when she had given birth was starting to get better.

Or, at least, visibly better. She knew that Beth had been complaining about the things she hadn't been able to do yet. Naomi wondered if her *schweschder* was just struggling with the fact that she didn't have anyone to help with Eli, or if she was truly still struggling with her mobility to some extent. Either way, she wasn't comfortable enough to comment. Especially not in front of their parents.

"Naomi! Where's the frosting?" Beth called from the other side of the bakery, interrupting Naomi's thoughts.

They were both in the rear, prepping orders for delivery that day. Beth was on frosting duty since her hands worked the best most often, and it kept her away from the heat of the ovens on the other side. Naomi was trying to prepare all of the frosting and stay on top of the dough that needed to rise, be rolled out, and put in the oven for the various sweets to be made.

Beth wanted cream cheese frosting since Naomi had just handed her a big pan of cinnamon rolls.

"It should be on the table, right beside the spatula," Naomi said. "Give me two seconds to finish getting this dough ready to proof and I can help you find it."

She kept her voice even and steady. It wouldn't help anyone to get upset with Beth. Since Eli was only just starting to sleep through the night, Beth was still struggling with sleep deprivation. It wasn't fair of Naomi to immediately think that Beth was doing this just to be difficult.

Sleep deprivation could make people do some weird things. It also impaired one's ability to see what was right in front of them. Naomi only knew this because of experiences from her *rumspringa*, and she wished that she didn't understand it this well sometimes.

Once she had put the dish towel over the bowl to let another batch of dough for cinnamon rolls rise, she turned to see if Beth had found the frosting. She found her *schweschder* massaging her wrists. It was probably fair to expect that her wrists were under some strain what with holding her *boppli*, feeding him, and helping in the bakery.

"Do you need a break from frosting, Beth?" Naomi asked gently.

She attempted to keep her tone from sounding accusatory. Beth had been incredibly touchy lately, perhaps because she felt as though she wasn't helping enough. However, this was only speculation on Naomi's part, but she could see how frustrated Beth was when she saw couples with a *boppli* at services and how happy and rested they looked.

Especially when the *daed* was holding said

boppli during the service and calming them down instead of allowing his *fraa* to do all of the work.

"*Nee*," Beth snapped. "I just need that frosting. It's not by the bowl, and since that-" here, Beth pointed to a large glass bowl, "-is the only bowl nearby, I'm not sure I understood it completely."

"...I swear I put the frosting there," Naomi said. "All right. I suppose it's time to find the frosting. This is going to be interesting."

She sighed. Instead of asking Beth if she had looked around the bowl or bothered to get up, Naomi went over to the table and found the frosting where she had left it. Sort of. It had been moved to the chair on the other side of the table at some point. Since she didn't remember doing it, and she knew that Beth hadn't done it, she wondered if their *daed* had.

"Here it is," Naomi said. "I think *Daed* moved it."

"That does sound like something he'd do," Beth replied with a soft sigh. "All right. How many of these do I need to frost? This looks like it'll cover the whole pan."

"If you need more, I'll make more," Naomi reminded her. "Unless an order comes in specifically for unfrosted, we're frosting them all this year."

Beth nodded.

"*Danke*," she said. "I don't know why I can't keep this all straight this year. Usually, this is where I excel."

"You have other things to worry about too, especially at home," Naomi said softly. "I'd think the first couple of Christmases that you're helping take all the orders here would be a little harder because you also have to remember how much you're doing at home."

Beth pursed her lips before starting to frost the cinnamon rolls. The practice was to frost the cinnamon rolls when they were hot. They didn't have to be hot out of the oven, but before they cooled down completely so that the frosting melted just a little. That little allowed the frosting to seep into each cinnamon roll which was the way the customers enjoyed them, they had learned.

With nothing currently in the oven, Naomi went ahead and made more frosting. It wasn't all that hard, since she'd had all the ingredients out already. The dough had more time to rise, but the frosting would be fine out on the counter while the goods baked. Besides that, if Beth wanted more frosting, there would be more ready.

It was then that Amos appeared in the back.

"We need another pan of cinnamon rolls up front. Immediately," he said. "Someone just ordered a pan, and they want them as soon as we can get it out. No frosting on any of them."

"I have a batch proofing and almost ready for the oven," Naomi said.

"*Ach*... if you had come five minutes earlier, we could have used this one," Beth said.

"They just ordered it. Five minutes ago, I didn't know," Amos said. "But that's all right. Naomi, when that batch is done in the oven, bring them to me immediately. I'll package them up."

"All right."

After checking on the dough, Naomi pulled the towel off the cinnamon rolls rising on the table and then she stuck them in the oven.

"I'm going to go take a quick walk," Naomi said. "Can you handle five or ten minutes in here without me?"

"Since those cinnamon rolls are going to take at least a half hour, I think so," Beth said. "Let *Daed* know."

Naomi nodded.

With that, she quietly told Amos where she was going and then left through the back door of the bakery.

NEW YEAR'S PROMISE

She wasn't so much going on a walk around the community as she was just going outside to clear her head. Watching Beth struggle with Eli and her personal problems – because Naomi was almost positive that she was still struggling with the reality of being alone for the foreseeable future – was making it hard to watch her struggle with helping in the bakery.

The cold winter air stung Naomi's lungs, but she was only outside for a couple of minutes.

When she went back inside, she found Beth in the front. After taking a quick look at the cinnamon rolls and the dough – both of which needed more time, as she had thought – she went to see what was going on.

Up front, she found Beth and her *daed* arguing with a customer. She only caught the tail end of the argument, but Naomi got the idea. The customer was upset that a few of the cinnamon rolls in his order were a little smushed. Once the customer had finished – and her *daed* had gotten him calmed down – Naomi walked over to Beth.

"How much frosting did you put on those cinnamon rolls?" Naomi asked. "They can't handle much!"

"It wasn't my fault!" Beth replied. "That bowl you put on the end of the table almost fell over and the only way to stop it from shattering was to catch it."

"And it landed right in the cinnamon rolls?"

"I… I may have tripped and caused it to fall…" Beth said, her face growing bright red.

Naomi walked into the rear of the bakery to prevent more of an argument, because she didn't want to attract the attention of more customers. She was acutely aware of everyone staring at them. Even her *daed* had been looking at her like she was crazy for attacking Beth for something that she couldn't control.

Naomi took in a deep breath.

It wasn't right of her to accuse her *schweschder* of doing wrong intentionally. She was still struggling with the changes that had come around because of Eli and giving birth. Beth was honestly doing her best and Naomi had just half-blown up at her for something that she probably couldn't control.

Beth had tripped for no apparent reason at home, too. Naomi had seen it happen.

She let out a sigh. Now was not the time to address it, but she still worried about Beth. How could she be tripping and struggling with mobility almost a year after she had given birth? It didn't make sense to Naomi.

CHAPTER 4

After the disaster at the bakery, Beth took a walk to calm down. Her *schweschder* yelling at her in front of the customers hadn't helped. In fact, it was starting to feel like the universe was actively trying to prevent her from healing after all that had happened the Christmas before.

Pulling her cloak closer to her body as a chilly wind blew, Beth happened to run into a *gut* friend's *mamm*: Anne King. Leah King, Anne's *dochder*, had been one of Beth's closest friends growing up. Now that she thought about it, she hadn't seen Leah around the community for a while. She wondered why.

"*Ach*. I'm sorry, Beth," Anne said as she realized who she had run into. "How have you been?

I hear you had quite a Christmas last year, delivering your little *boppli* in the barn."

"Quite a Christmas indeed," Beth replied. "It's been a slow recovery. How have you and Leah been? I've not seen her around the community for a while. Is she all right?"

She didn't think she could take learning that another person so dear to her heart had passed on, but her curiosity was too much to prevent her from opening her mouth. However, there was nothing more for her to do but wait for Anne's answer. It appeared Anne didn't know how to answer her. Instead of answering immediately, Anne pursed her lips. That was never a *gut* sign.

Anne King was one of those people in the community who was a pillar of hope. If there was a disaster in the community, Beth and others had often joked that Anne King would find a way to see the best in the situation and bring the entire community some levity. The silence from her brought no levity now.

"Well, you see... Leah's been shunned," Anne finally said. "I don't know what else to tell you. She's been found to be out of line with the community's way of life, and she's not sure how to correct it because she doesn't see anything wrong with what she's done."

"What do you mean, she doesn't see anything wrong?" Beth furrowed her eyebrows, unsure of what this was supposed to mean.

There were plenty of reasons for one to be shunned, and Beth could easily list them. They were all willful acts of refusing to repent that led to shunning, but certain sins couldn't be forgiven immediately. Atonement had to be shown before a shunning could end. She hoped that Leah hadn't been shunned for one of the more serious sins.

"She's been courting an *Englischer* who appears to have no interest in converting," Anne replied. "And she is much in love. Too much in love to see what she is choosing to do instead of weighing her options by who is most important to her." Anne shook her head. "I have to worry that my *dochder* may end up leaving and be unallowed to return. I have asked why she accepted the courtship, but she insists the community has it wrong. Refuses to further elaborate."

"That is indeed a heavy worry," Beth said.

Her heart sank a little. Hearing that her friend was being shunned was hard, but to hear that it was because she didn't want to give up on seeing if her relationship would work was worse. Sometimes, things were going on behind the scenes of a relationship that only the couple knew. She knew that there had been times when her *familye* had been concerned for her as Jacob had traveled so often for work, but there had been an agreement about how he was to travel and why. And how he was supposed to let her know that he was traveling for work.

It also brought up something she had never thought of before, being a new *mamm*: what would happen if her *sohn* was in a position where he was shunned? Would she risk also being shunned by the community to support Eli, or would she ask that he reconsider his actions? Would it have mattered at any point?

"I'm sorry if any of this worries you. You have enough on your plate already, and here I am adding to it," Anne said upon seeing the look on Beth's face. "I should be going. I have a meal to prepare."

Beth nodded slowly and continued on her walk. As much as she wanted to help Leah see that she was risking everything for a *mann* who may not want her if she didn't leave the community, she was afraid of getting shunned herself. She needed all the help she could get right now.

If she helped Leah, there was a *gut* chance that the elders of the community would enforce shunning on her, leaving Eli with her parents and

Naomi to be looked after. Or worse, forcing her to take Eli with her because they didn't want her here at all.

As she continued to walk, she meandered into the center of the community. The bakery was close enough to the center that it wasn't so far-fetched to end up here on a walk to cool off.

"Beth?"

A voice interrupted the painful thoughts of agonizing over the future, and she turned to see who had spoken to her. Just a few feet away – and getting closer – she saw Samuel. She couldn't recall his last name off the top of her head, but then, she didn't think it mattered.

The sturdily built man was walking towards her and in this weather, she almost missed noticing his beard. It had started graying, looking more like salt and pepper as the *Englischers* might have called it. However, his kind eyes were staring at her.

"I hope I haven't interrupted anything important," he said as he caught up to her. "How are you today, Beth?"

"I'm doing all right," she said, not wanting him to feel as though he had to make things better. "And yourself?"

"I'm doing all right myself," he said. "As are my

kinner, this holiday season. It sure has gotten cold this year."

Beth nodded.

Samuel had been no stranger to her over the last year. He had two small *kinner* himself – Irene and Daniel. His late *fraa* had been an *Englischer* who converted, and to honor her *mamm,* they had named their eldest after her. It was a beautiful if odd name to find in the Amish community. However, it wasn't because of his *kinner* or the fact that he was a widower that he had been no stranger to her.

He had been subtly trying to initiate a courtship with her for the better part of the last six months. She supposed that he was trying to do so subtly because he didn't know if she was ready, but she was not up to courting right now. Her husband's death was still far too recent.

"It gets cold every winter, Samuel," Beth finally said upon realizing that he was waiting for a response. "Can I help you?"

"Are you walking home?"

"*Nee.*"

"Perhaps I could walk you back to the bakery then? I've heard about how the cold makes your injuries act up," he said.

Beth looked at him, earnestly searching for

any sign that he was trying to start something more than just being sweet. She supposed he would have been a great *daed* for Eli, but she was not sure how she would even start going about looking for a way to make that happen.

"I'll be all right walking back on my own," Beth said. "Besides, I've yet to accomplish my errand. I'm coming for more spices."

"*Ach*."

Samuel moved out of her way since they were rather close to the general store. Beth was not running an errand for more spices for the bakery, but now that she had said that she was, they did need more cinnamon. Those cinnamon rolls required a lot, especially at this time of year.

"But I appreciate the offer," Beth continued. "I'll be all right. Go tend to your *kinner*, if you can."

Samuel nodded slowly and walked away. Though he didn't show it on his face, she could tell by the slump of his head and shoulders that he was upset about not being able to escort her back to the bakery.

Beth had been extremely careful so far not to let any of the single *menner* in the community walk with her. There was an active gossip mill, and with the way they were going on about

Naomi still not belonging in the community – even after being baptized and marrying Isaac – she didn't want to become the next focus. There was plenty for the community to worry about besides her.

As she walked into the general store, she shook her head. This wasn't the time to be thinking fo the gossip mill. Instead, she got a few containers of cinnamon since they were rather small. Perhaps it had to do with the time of year.

After paying for her cinnamon, she stuck the bottles in the pockets of her apron and headed back to the bakery. Samuel had long since fled from sight, which meant that she didn't have to worry about him asking again if he could escort her on her walk.

As much as she wanted to accept his offer and the courtship it might have initiated, she still felt far too much love in her heart for Jacob to be able to move on.

CHAPTER 5

Upon arriving home that evening, Beth found herself gravitating towards caring for Eli. There was something about the innocence of a *boppli* too young to care for himself that she needed right now. It made her feel as though she was at least appreciated by one person. In a sea of people who seemed all too concerned with Eli's well-being and not hers, she appreciated that Eli couldn't ask how she was doing. Instead, he seemed to laugh and babble at her as if he knew all of her troubles and worries. She knew it wasn't that simple, though.

He was laughing and babbling because that's what children his age did. She'd seen enough of her friends have *kinner* that she was aware of how fast they learned, and when to start worrying that they weren't learning how to interact with the world around them fast enough.

As she sat with him at the window, she watched the snow fall to the ground. Every time he giggled and clapped his hands at the glass, she felt her heart lift just a little. Although this season was fraught with guilt about having to raise a *boppli* alone and the grief of not knowing how to spend the holidays without her husband, she was glad to have this little bright spot.

Beth admitted she found it rather funny when Eli reached out to touch the window and got excited, which resulted in him hitting the window. But she did her best not to laugh. She had a feeling that her parents wouldn't appreciate the sound of him doing it over and over.

"*Ach*, don't let him hit the window!" Clara said, interrupting Beth's thoughts.

"Why not? It's cold, and he likes the experience. I'm right here if he gets too cold," Beth said, turning to face her *mamm* for a moment before turning back to Eli. "Besides, he's watching the snow fall. Aren't you, Eli? Aren't you?"

Eli let out another small laugh as he clapped, just watching the snow fall.

"He'll smear the glass," Clara said sternly. "I

didn't let you or Naomi anywhere near the windows like that until you knew that you couldn't touch them."

"*Mamm*. He's not even a year old yet. Almost, though. He'll be all right."

"*Mamm!*" With that, Eli started babbling again, and this time, he said a word.

While it wasn't new by any means, Eli calling her '*mamm*' was a reminder of how much light she brought to his life, even if she didn't feel it some days. She supposed it was a good way to remind herself that there was always going to be a reason to keep going now.

"I don't want him by the window until he's at least five or six. Not on his own," Clara continued. "It's the principle of it. Smears are hard to wash off of the glass."

"He's not hurting you or the glass by hitting it," she said. "Not like that anyway. It's like us pointing to the snow when it fell each year. I'm just continuing that tradition, I suppose."

Her *mamm* made a disapproving sound, but that was the end of the conversation. As Clara walked away, Beth felt a little smaller. She had just started feeling like she was doing something right, letting Eli watch the snow fall while she let her back and legs rest after all the business of the holiday season. Why did her *mamm* have to make her feel as though the joy she felt from watching Eli get excited over his first snowfall was bad?

"*Ach*, Eli," Beth said as she watched him, making sure he didn't fall. "Whatever will I do with the memories I have of doing this as a *kind* and my wish to make sure that you have the same memories? That you at least get the chance to make them? Do I need to start finding a way to move on from Jacob and the grief I still feel over him?"

She knew that Eli wouldn't have the answers, but it made her feel better to ask out loud anyway. All Eli did in response was giggle and blow a raspberry at her before pointing at the snow.

He looked back at her.

"That's snow, Eli," she said. "Snow."

He attempted to say the word with her, but he had been having trouble with the sound of the letter 'S' for a while. He'd be able to say it right, eventually. She just had to be patient. That word brought the argument she'd just had with her *mamm* to mind.

Patience was not plentiful at this time of year with her parents. Then again, she knew that the bakery took up a lot of their time. To have to take care of Eli as well probably only exacerbated the issues, especially since they hadn't planned on offering so much help when Beth had gotten married.

Eli started to yawn, rubbing at his eyes.

"All right. If you're tired, let's put you down for a nap," Beth said. "*Kumm* on."

She sat Eli on the floor and let him get around as he pleased. He toddled alongside her, holding onto the hem of her skirt to get around. She found it quite cute. If he trusted her enough to be able to walk alongside her like that, she would not do anything that would jeopardize that trust.

He plopped down on the floor halfway to the room where he would be sleeping. He rubbed his eyes again before lying down on the floor.

Considering this was a high-traffic hallway, Beth decided that she wasn't going to allow him to fall asleep there. Instead, she bent down and picked him up.

"All right, all right," she said with a soft laugh. "You can't lie down in the middle of the hallway. I don't want you getting hurt. Let's get you to bed where you'll be safe. I'd feel guilty if something happened to you because you were sleeping in the middle of the hallway when I know that there's going to be a lot of people going up and down past you."

Eli just snuggled his head into her shoulder and let out a yawn.

Beth took him into the room they were sharing for the time being and put him down for a nap. He didn't have to settle for long before he was fast asleep. Beth looked at her *sohn* in the crib and smiled.

There was no reason that he shouldn't touch the window or hit it while enjoying the sight of the snow falling outside. He had not been malicious in hitting the window. Not today, anyway. And watching him in his crib reminded her that he knew very little of right and wrong at the moment. She'd teach him, though. She promised herself that before walking out of the room.

When she returned to the living room, she found both her parents waiting for her. This didn't look *gut*. Her *mamm* was frowning deeply at her, while her *daed* simply looked displeased. She wondered why. Although she and Naomi had grown up with stricter discipline than most had in the community, she didn't think Eli needed to be parented in that way.

"That boy is going to grow up not knowing right from wrong if you don't start showing him," her *daed* said. "*Kinner* need a *gut*, strong, guiding hand this early in life. Why aren't you providing that?"

"I've decided I don't want to parent Eli as you parented me and Naomi," Beth said quietly, hoping that she could head off an argument before it woke Eli. "I want to give him a gentle guiding hand. My friends recommend it. It's a harder route to go when you're angry with your *kinner*, but I think Eli deserves to have a gentler upbringing than I remember, or than his late *daed* had."

She had always wondered if it was a miracle that Jacob hadn't turned to alcohol sooner given that his parents had been so strict on him. She didn't want Eli to be struggling with the same sins, and one of the best ways to change that outcome was to avoid giving him reasons to drink like Jacob had.

She was not physically disciplined but it had left her wondering some nights if her parents truly loved her or if they were just trying to make sure that she didn't make their life harder.

"He'll grow up to leave the community if you do that!" Clara said, breaking Beth out of her thoughts. "You need to provide him a steady, firm hand in guidance."

"I'm pretty sure that the only reason he'd leave

the community is because he feels more at home in the city than he ever did here," Beth replied, her voice rising a little. "And if I can give him a loving home, then I will be preventing him from having those feelings. Don't you see that there are multiple ways to get to the same destination when it comes to parenting?"

"This wouldn't be happening if Jacob was still alive," Amos spat at her.

Her *daed's* words cut deep. Beth walked out of the room before she could say anything that she'd regret and disappeared into her room.

Eli was fast asleep, which was all that mattered to her. She sat on her bed, grabbed a pillow, and buried her face in it as the tears started to run. How could her *daed* say that to her?

CHAPTER 6

Naomi had gone to a quilting circle to help get her mind off of the letters she had found in the closet. It was usually a source of gossip, and today, she was rather thankful for that. Anything was better than thinking about the fact that Isaac had kept letters from the woman he once courted.

However, as she was working on a quilt to gift Eli at Christmas, she heard some of the other ladies whispering.

"What has your attention over there?" She looked over at them, knowing that the gossip always started small like that.

"I'm sure you remember my *dochder*, Hannah," one of the women, Sarah Glick, said. "Well, she's decided that this year, she's going to *kumm* home for the holidays. Isn't that exciting?" She smiled widely.

Naomi's breathing hitched. While the name Hannah was popular in the community, she had now realized that she didn't know the last name of the Hannah whom Isaac previously courted. Perhaps not knowing it was for the best. She didn't think she could handle knowing that Hannah Glick wrote such letters to Isaac so many years ago.

"I have met many Hannahs while living here," Naomi said. "I'm sorry. I don't think I've met her. Perhaps I could meet her this holiday season."

"Huh. I could have sworn you would have met her," Sarah said. "You and she went out for your *Rumspringa* around the same time. She sent a letter to the young *mann* she was courting at the time stating that she was going to be leaving the community shortly after she left as she had found another community that agreed with her better. I can't recall who she was courting at the time. I do remember it devastated us all when we learned Hannah wasn't returning."

This caused Naomi's heart to sink. That was suspiciously similar to the story that Isaac had told her about how the relationship with Hannah had ended. It still didn't answer why he had kept the letters, but she supposed that there was no accounting for actions made due to a broken heart.

"I... I don't think we ever met, *nee*," Naomi finally managed to say, breaking out of her thoughts. "But she sounds like she must not have been very happy here."

She had only added the last part to keep herself from feeling like she needed to wallow in pity. There was no reason for her to feel that Isaac would have any interest in Hannah now that they were married. However, hearing how Hannah's life had turned out was not making it any easier to be present at the quilting circle.

She wondered if some of the other women had picked up on it because Sarah said no more about Hannah, bar a shrug that she had been unhappy living there.

Regardless, Naomi finished the square she had been working on, gathered her supplies, and left the barn. She didn't want to hear anything more about Hannah and what her plans were for the holidays. Besides, it was right before Eli's birthday, too. She couldn't believe that this was all happening at once.

Why couldn't her *familye* just get one year to be normal, to celebrate the holidays without worrying? Or were they doomed to spend all the holidays going forward worrying about the fragile structure that had been set up after Jacob's death and her marriage to Isaac?

When she returned home, she found that Isaac was home. That wasn't unusual on a weekend. He only worked during the week, and if he was going to work a weekend, it'd be in the summer when there was a need for it. Especially since with the snow falling, there was no need for him to be making deliveries right now. If they wanted more help, they could find it – or they could make sure that Beth was home to watch Eli so that her parents were there to help.

"How was the quilting circle, Naomi?" Isaac asked upon realizing that she had come home.

"It was *gut*," Naomi replied.

She didn't know why, but she was still struggling to comprehend the fact that Hannah might be returning to the community. Her *mamm* seemed incredibly sure but using the words 'might' and 'maybe' made her feel at least a little less threatened. She didn't know exactly why, but Naomi supposed it was because she was wondering if there was a chance Isaac would leave her for Hannah after her reappearance in the community.

"Well, the bakery's all in one piece. I've not yet gotten word on the bakery's annex from the council, but I hope that it'll pass," he continued. "Now, why don't we have some time to ourselves? I'm sure there's going to be plenty of time to worry about the annex later, and if it goes through, we'll have to worry about all the details that *kumm* with putting that plan into action."

He approached her, putting an arm around her shoulders. For some reason, Naomi pulled away. She didn't know how to tell him that she wasn't feeling like physical affection today, or that she just needed some time to process her emotions.

"Naomi?"

Isaac sounded rather upset, but she didn't know what else to do. The thought of being around him right now was not one she wished to entertain right now, despite living with him.

"I'm just exhausted," she said as she took another step toward the bedroom. "The quilting circle was far more work than I've put into a quilt lately, and I think I overworked myself. I think a nap will set me right."

He nodded slowly.

"Then I hope you have a *gut* nap. I'll be here when you're ready," he said. "Do you want me to do anything around the *haus* while you're napping?"

"If you could at least make sure we've got things for lunch and dinner for the week, that'd be *Wunderbar*. I think the snow's going to continue. If we need things, now is the time to go to the general store and get them," she mused.

"All right."

With that, Naomi made it into the bedroom without much else to say. She shut the door behind her, but that was only out of habit. They often slept with the bedroom door closed, and she didn't think he'd mind it closed while she took a nap.

As much as she wanted to take a nap, Naomi was far too energized to sleep. Excited was certainly the wrong word for how she felt, but she couldn't help but liken the way the energy was flowing through her to being excited. Perhaps anxious was the better word. She didn't like that there were rumors at the quilting circle that Hannah Glick was returning to the community, but since Isaac had married Naomi – not Hannah – she didn't think she should have had any reason to worry.

Regardless, she lay on the bed, not knowing what else to do. She did take her shoes off as they were dirty and more than likely the treads would be caked with snow. Melted snow from her shoe was not a *gut* idea on the bed without a fire going to dry it out.

Thanks to the snow outside, the bedroom was rather cold. She didn't think that Isaac was going to start a fire, as there was one dying in the fireplace and he was planning to go to the general store now that she had suggested it. Then again, she didn't mind that the bedroom was cold. There were plenty of quilts on the bed for this reason.

That, and it wasn't always a *gut* idea to leave a fire going at night.

As she heard the door shut – meaning she was right and that Isaac was going to head to the general store– she crawled under the blankets. She didn't think that it was right of her to lie to Isaac and decided to at least try to take a nap.

Naomi closed her eyes.

However, all that she could see or hear as she attempted to nap was what might happen if Hannah were to show up for the holidays. She saw Isaac leaving her for Hannah, who had had so much love in her heart for him that he had retained enough love to make it worth the shunning that he would get from the community.

It didn't make sense to her, but that was her only worry. That he would realize he had given up something *Wunderbar* in Hannah and had made a mistake in allowing her to leave without pursuing her in her new community.

After about a half hour of this, she decided that she wasn't going to be getting a nap after all, and she got up to stoke the fire in the living room. It hadn't completely died out yet, but it was close. The embers caught on the papers she threw in, and she imagined throwing the letters from Hannah into the fire.

It wasn't the most mature thing to do – imagining that she was destroying his property – but it was the only thing that allowed her heart to stop racing.

In front of the fire, she sat on the couch. She pulled the quilt from the back of the couch, curled up, and fell asleep there instead of in their bed. Now that her jealousy had been somewhat contained, sleep came easily to her.

CHAPTER 7

A couple of days later, Beth and Samuel were walking along the pathways in the community. She wasn't sure of the plan, but she was enjoying his company. Despite his wish to court her, he was a *gut* friend. That was the only reason she hadn't stopped seeing him. She didn't want to lose a *gut* friend over her inability to get over Jacob. If he persisted, she would make sure that he understood that he was risking their friendship.

"What do you do when Eli does something you don't want him to do?" Samuel asked.

She wasn't sure why he was inquisitive about her parenting, but she supposed it was only because this time last year she had expressed that she wasn't sure what kind of parent she was going to be. Perhaps it was his way of seeing if she was open to parenting advice. That was honestly the last thing she wanted after her experiences with her parents, but she supposed it didn't hurt to hear more than one opinion on the matter.

"I tell him *nee*, and I give him an explanation of why," Beth replied. "I try not to just tell him 'because I said so'. I was told that so many times as a *kind*, and I didn't like it too much. I think Eli deserves more than that."

Samuel nodded slowly.

"That's one way of doing it, *jah*," he said. "Does he understand what you're saying?"

"I don't think so," she admitted with a bit of a laugh. "At least, not yet. He's not yet a year old, after all. I think, in time, he will start to understand what I'm saying. If I start now, while he can't understand me, I'm only building the expectation. Makes it easier to do when he can understand me. Hopefully."

Samuel laughed.

"I can see why you would want to build the expectation if you're not used to it," he said. "My *kinner* have a few rules that I've instated in the home that are there for their protection, but they only listen if I say 'because I said so.' I don't know

NEW YEAR'S PROMISE

why." He shook his head. "Maybe it's because of their age. They're exploring their world and don't like to be told that they can't explore something that looks so *gut* to them."

"I imagine I may have the same issue with Eli," Beth admitted. "However, I refuse to tell him that it's a rule simply because I said so. He deserves to know that it's for his protection, to make sure that nothing bad happens."

"How do you plan to handle him when he starts courting? It's the most difficult part of parenting here, I hear. That or if he decides he wants to leave the community," Samuel speculated.

"I'll make sure that he understands you do not mess with a woman's heart," she said. "Courting is a commitment not just of one's time, but of one's heart."

"Not when he just begins, I'd say," Samuel argued. "When *kinner* just begin to court – no matter what age it is – they're not courting to find a husband or a *fraa*. They're courting to get used to it. You do know that the first courtship is usually not the one that they end up marrying, *jah*?"

"I'm well aware of that, Samuel," Beth replied, somewhat harshly. "I think it would be better for him to know that he is not to mess with a woman's heart and be upfront about his intentions for a courtship than it would be for him to accidentally break someone's heart. That's never fun nor easy to get over, either."

She pursed her lips as Samuel fell quiet. She understood that she had a different view of parenting than many in the community, but was it honestly that different? Was it so odd to think that her *kinner* deserved to know that they were loved, but that there were things that they shouldn't do because it would hurt others and not just because it was a bad thing to do?

Or had she been more influenced by the *Englischers* than she had thought during her *rumspringa*?

"That's an interesting philosophy," he finally said. "I think that comes more from *Englischers* than it does our own community. Are you sure you're doing all right raising Eli by yourself?" He pursed his lips and furrowed his eyebrows.

Beth frowned deeply. How dare he imply that she was doing wrong by her *sohn's* upbringing!

"I'm raising Eli fine all by myself, *danke*," she said sternly. "I don't need to be arguing parenting styles with you. I'm already having this argument with my parents. Why does everyone feel that I must explain myself to them with what I'm doing to discipline Eli?"

She pursed her lips. She didn't like having to explain what she was doing all the time. However, she supposed that most of the people in the community were just asking because they cared.

"Beth, it's not that we don't think you don't know what you're doing," Samuel started, "but that we want to be sure that you're coping. You're all alone, parenting a *kind*. Or, at least, that's how I'm approaching it. Am I wrong to think that it might be nice to have someone there who could offer you some advice if you need it?"

She looked at him. The way he had pursed his lips, furrowed his eyebrows, and the look he was currently giving her all spoke of concern. But she didn't feel that he was all that concerned. All she felt was that he wanted to be able to give his advice on parenting, whether she wanted to hear it or not.

"I'm not sure," she finally said.

She didn't entirely want to share with him that she was not interested in hearing the critiques he had about her, but she wanted to scream it from the heavens. She'd heard enough criticism of her parenting to last a lifetime in just this last year. However, some part of her suspected that it was not about to end just because she did not appreciate it.

"*Ach.*"

He did stop there, thankfully. She wasn't sure what she would have said if he continued to tell her what was appropriate and what wasn't.

When their walk ended, Beth returned home. He probably meant well, but she didn't want to hear it. It just wasn't helpful, especially when she felt that the entire community was watching her to see how she was taking care of Eli after the death of Jacob.

Upon arriving home, she went to see Eli. He was taking a nap, so there was nothing useful she could do there. Instead of going to see what she could do for her parents, she took in a deep breath and watched her *sohn* sleep for a few minutes. He looked so innocent.

It was at this moment that she decided that she was not going to listen to the advice other parents were giving her. Something about raising Eli with the same rigid rules she had been raised with didn't sit right with her. While she would consider the advice she was given, that didn't mean that she would put it all into use.

But Samuel's words echoed in her head: "Am I wrong to think that it might be nice to have someone there who could offer you some advice if you need it?"

She didn't need it. Not from someone who was blindly following the same parenting style they had been raised by. She didn't think it was proper. There needed to be a way forward that included learning from mistakes. Not just repeating those same mistakes until they were considered the right way to do things.

She didn't think it was going to happen, and she started to wonder if she was doing right by Eli. At his age, all *kinner* reacted more or less the same to being told they couldn't do something depending on how much they wanted to do it. She supposed some parents immediately assumed their *kinner* were doing their best to make their lives difficult.

That's not how Beth saw it. The way she saw it, Eli had never been this age before. He deserved a chance to learn from his mistakes without someone immediately believing that he was going to sin just because she refused to always be strict with him. There were a few things that she would share with him when he got older in hopes that he wouldn't repeat the same mistakes she and Jacob had made – one of those being Jacob's alcoholism and her assuming that he could handle it by himself.

She certainly didn't think that was being strict. After all, she wanted him to learn that no matter what the community said about his actions, she would find a way to help him out of a bad situation. Even if it risked her own status in the community. After all, what kind of a parent would she be if she put the community's rules and rigidity above the well-being of her own *kind*?

"I swear to you, Eli, I'll raise you right. If it's the last thing I do right," she whispered as she started towards the door. "I just hope the rest of the community realizes that's what I'm doing before they run us both out of the community."

With that, she walked into the dining room to see what she could do to help.

CHAPTER 8

They had finally received feedback from the council about the annex proposal for the bakery. They wanted to extend the bakery because they were struggling to keep up with the demand right now. If they had more room in the rear for ovens, mixing, stoves, and the like, they would be able to better serve the community. Not to mention the amount of *Englischer* traffic that came through at this time of year because they had somehow come to be features on the GPS apps.

Naomi wasn't sure what it meant to the *Englischers* who came, but she knew that it meant the bakery was packed at this time of year.

Unfortunately, the council rejected the annex

proposal. Staring at the paper that read "Rejected" in her hands, Naomi didn't know what else to do. She and Isaac needed this to happen. There was just no other way they were going to be able to survive in the community, and it hurt to know that so little consideration was given about their ability to survive that their application had been rejected.

Instead of immediately beginning to despair, Naomi read through the paper. Usually, when the council issued a rejection, they listed their concerns, and gave a date to resubmit an application that addressed concerns.

Their letter stated the council's concerns about increased *Englisch* foot traffic disrupting the community's tranquility. As if this was an acceptable reason to prevent them from getting a little more room in the back. She didn't understand it.

Not all *Englischers* were awful. Some had been awful in the context of what was going on around the bakery, but those who came specifically for the bakery's treats weren't exactly interested in exploring the rest of the community. She was beginning to think her *daed* had been smart when he had set up the bakery near the road which most *Englischers* used to drive into the community. If they were just looking for a place to stretch, get some food and a beverage, and then be on their way, the bakery was perfectly situated.

Naomi sat back when she realized that there wasn't much she could actually do to alleviate that worry. The *Englischers* talked in the lobby while they were waiting for their treats, there appeared to be quite the interest in niche, *familye*-owned bakeries among those who were called 'foodies' right now. That was part of the reason their bakery was so popular.

Besides, the more money they brought into the bakery, the more there would be to spread around if they didn't have *kinner* soon. There was always a reason to need money around here, especially in winter. Was the council so worried that the extra foot traffic would further disrupt the peace that they'd rather Naomi and Isaac just find another way to earn a living? Maybe by selling more crafts or baked goods at the Christmas Market, which was one of the few times of year that the council appeared all right with so many *Englischers* in the community?

Isaac walked through the front door, interrupting her musing, and Naomi put the paper down on the table in front of her. If he wasn't already aware, she was not excited to tell him the update about the annex.

The fact that they were worried about increased *Englischer* traffic made her wonder if her past mistakes on her *rumspringa* had anything to do with the decision to reject the annex. If that was true, then why couldn't people learn to accept that she had made mistakes and she was repenting of them daily? And it still wasn't enough.

"*Hallo*, Naomi," Isaac said as he walked into the room.

She wondered how he had come to have signs of flour in his blond hair. Whatever the case, he clearly had something on his mind. He didn't normally come home so messy after a day at the bakery. Naomi had not been in the bakery today because she had been taking care of the *haus*, but she desperately wanted to be there. She saw it as a coping mechanism of sorts, and staying away was driving her crazy.

"*Hallo*. What happened to your hair?" she looked up, trying to be subtle.

His face flushed, and he began shaking the flour out of his hair.

"I fell while carrying a bag of flour. I think my hair held onto the flour the best, but that's neither here nor there," he replied. "Have you received

NEW YEAR'S PROMISE

the council's decision about the annex? I hear they made their decision today. One of the council members came into the bakery. Wouldn't talk about it, but he did appear somewhat... forlorn about it."

"I got it, all right," Naomi said. "They rejected it. What are we to do, Isaac?"

"Don't despair," Isaac said softly, putting a hand on hers.

She pulled her hand away. She didn't know what to do or say, but she knew that the last thing she wanted was Isaac's comfort. There was still a sting over the fact that he had kept those letters from his past and that this Hannah might be around for the holidays. But she believed he didn't need to know that.

"We'll figure out how to fix this. We need that annex," he continued. "Did they at least give a reason? That would be a tremendous help in finding a way around their rejection."

"They're worried that an annex would allow for more *Englischer* foot traffic, thus disrupting the tranquility of the community even further. It's not like the bakery's right by the general store, for goodness sakes!"

Naomi couldn't help but allow her voice to rise a little. She had thought she was doing so well in getting along within the community again, but this had just reminded her that no matter what she did, she might as well have remained in the city.

"Easy, Naomi. It's not your fault that the community council is worried about that. I'm sure they've had some complaints because not all of the *Englischers* coming through our bakery are the nicest," he said softly. "And this is why they can't have nice things, I hear. Others ruin it for them. Do you have an idea of what we can do to get around this? To revise the plan to be in line with what they'd expect?"

"*Nee*," Naomi admitted.

"Then you cannot despair yet, because we have not explored all our options," Isaac said simply. "Please, let me help you write the next one."

Naomi took in a deep breath before nodding slowly.

But she didn't accept the hug he offered with his arms outstretched to her. Instead, she walked past him and into the kitchen. There were more chores to be done in the *haus* before they went to bed. And she intended to get them done.

"What is going on with you lately, Naomi?" Isaac asked as he followed her into the kitchen. "Why do you blow off my attempts to comfort you? You usually love to get hugs when I *kumm* back from the bakery. You say I smell of the bread we bake. What is going on?"

"I just don't want a hug right now." Naomi didn't know what else to say.

How would Isaac respond if he learned that she was jealous of Hannah, of the way he still so tenderly cared for the letters that Hannah had sent while they were courting? Would he understand how it looked to her? Or would he think she was slightly crazy for feeling that way?

"*Ach.*"

Isaac appeared to understand that she didn't want a hug more than anything else right now. That was exactly how she wanted to leave it, but she wasn't sure that he was going to appreciate anything more tonight.

"I know it's unusual, but I think I'm just a little worn out. I'm sure it'll be better tomorrow," she said.

He wasn't the one in need of reassurance, really, but she didn't want him pressing to find out why she didn't want hugs. That would have been embarrassing, she thought. Especially when she wasn't ready to share what was going on in her head.

"Then why don't I take care of dinner tonight?" Isaac offered.

"You've been on your feet all day. I can handle dinner," Naomi rebuffed.

He nodded and went to sit at the dining room table. While it hurt to tell him that she didn't need his comfort, her jealousy was hers to deal with, and hers alone. However, that wasn't what was most concerning to her right now.

With the council having rejected the bakery annex, she worried about the future in the community for herself and Isaac. Had she been right last year when she had thought that marrying or courting Isaac would only get his name dragged through the mud as well by association with her? Or was this worry something they always had to keep in mind when submitting to the council?

CHAPTER 9

It wasn't until a Christmas event – a large dinner – that Beth decided that she was going to give Samuel another chance. She had been avoiding him since their last conversation about parenting struggles had given her a reason to feel that he didn't have her best interests at heart. But Christmas was all about new beginnings. Perhaps she could find it in her heart to let him in, even if only for a friendship, this year.

It was awfully lonely as a single parent. He would know that sting better than anyone in the community because he was a widower. It wasn't the same, as she knew that the love between Samuel and his late *fraa* had been great, but it was all she had to relate to in the community right now.

With Eli safe in Clara's arms, Beth made her way towards Samuel. They were all gathered in a large barn that had been constructed for the purpose of hosting large community gatherings during the winter. It also served as a venue for the youth to gather on Sunday nights for singings.

"*Hallo*, Beth," Samuel said with a smile when she arrived. "I'm glad to see that you made it tonight. I was beginning to wonder if I was going to see you here at all. If I said anything that rubbed you the wrong way the last time we talked, I'm sorry. It wasn't my intention."

"*Danke* for the apology," Beth replied. "It wasn't your fault it rubbed me the wrong way. Many people have been questioning whether I know what's best for Eli. I'd had enough. It wasn't right of me to explode like that on you. The straw that broke the camel's back, and all that, you know."

Part of why she had *kumm* today was because she felt that she owed Samuel an apology. She'd made a mistake. And how was her *sohn* ever going to learn that it was right to admit to mistakes if he didn't know that his *mamm* did it, too?

"Well, since you're here, why don't you sit with me?" Samuel asked, motioning to one of the free seats at his table. "I'm sure you'd like to have some company apart from your parents for a change. Or your *schweschder,* as sweet as Naomi and Isaac are together."

Beth smiled a little. Samuel appeared to be on point with everything he was saying tonight. She wasn't sure whether that was because he just didn't want to run her off again or because he had given it some serious thought. But she did know that she appreciated being with someone outside of her *familye.*

"And where are your *kinner* tonight?" Beth asked, curious.

It was rare to see him without the *kinner,* although he could have said the same of her when she wasn't working in the bakery. Some days, her parents simply insisted that she be able to go out and have some time with her friends. That was partially what was happening tonight, and she was thankful. It meant that she could have some fun without having to worry about who would find Eli's crying annoying and offering her advice she didn't appreciate.

"They're with my parents. They're both a little under the weather, what with it being so cold,"

Samuel admitted. "But my parents thought that it'd be *gut* for me to get out of the *haus* for a few hours. I don't think I've caught what they have, but I'm willing to stay a few feet away if you'd feel more comfortable with that."

"I don't mind," she replied. "Besides, I have a feeling that a few here have gotten ill in the last little while. It's winter season. Colds are going around like it's no one's business. I have always hated that part of the Christmas season. So long as Eli doesn't get sick, I don't mind."

Samuel smiled.

"That's a *gut* response, I think," he said.

They started discussing the various troubles they experienced as single parents, and Beth felt her heart starting to warm. Perhaps her parents had been right: all she needed to do was find someone she could share her struggles with. Someone who would understand why she wanted to have someone beside her. She wasn't entirely certain she wanted to trust him completely yet but that would *kumm* in time.

Eventually, she moved away from Samuel to get some food. While she was in the line, she realized that the town gossips were only a few people in front of her. And their voices carried better than a bird's song in the snow.

"Did you hear that Leah King has had a friendship with an *Englisch* shop owner?" one of them said. "How scandalous! No wonder she's been shunned. If that were to develop into something more, what kind of community would we be? We certainly wouldn't be only Amish, and I don't like the sound of that."

"I heard that it had already gotten that far, and that's why it's inappropriate," the other replied. "Leah King, with an *Englischer!* Can you believe the nerve of her? Did she not learn from watching Naomi Fisher make the same mistakes on her *rumspringa* when she had a chance to repent and still struggled to get a place in the community? I don't pity the woman. She deserves to be shunned."

Beth couldn't listen to more of that gossip and attempted to pretend that she wasn't listening. Some of the women in the community found far too much joy in making sure that the community followed the rules as rigidly as possible, and that wasn't doing anyone any *gut*. Especially not those who wanted to return to the community but felt that they had no place.

She'd seen how it had affected Naomi, and she hadn't known what to do then, either. Now, she at least knew that there were consequences for trying to help Leah. Beth didn't really care at this point, though. If they were going to shun her friend, perhaps she could talk some sense into Leah. She shook those thoughts away, though, as she finished getting her food.

Once her plate was full, Beth returned to Samuel at the table. He was talking to some of his friends, so she sat down quietly beside him.

However, instead of listening attentively as she ate, Beth couldn't help but worry about how isolated Leah might be feeling, a thought brought around by the gossip she'd heard earlier. Although Beth had never been shunned, she had a feeling that the isolation wasn't doing her friend any *gut*. Especially if the community gossip thought that it would prevent the gossip from getting to her. That wasn't how it worked.

Beth knew from Naomi's experience of being shunned and gossiped about that Leah would eventually hear the gossip about herself. And it wouldn't hit softly. It'd hit all at once, and it wouldn't be easy to forget once it had been heard. She was acutely aware that Naomi still struggled to feel like part of the community, despite having repented and *kumm* back to the teachings as soon as she realized what a mistake she'd made.

It had almost robbed her *schweschder* of the

happiness of marriage. She didn't want to see Leah go through the same thing.

"Don't you think, Beth?"

Suddenly being addressed pulled her out of her thoughts. She looked up from her food only to find Samuel looking at her as if he was expecting an answer.

"I'm sorry. I don't think I caught the question," she admitted. "What did you ask?"

"A shame that Leah King isn't here, don't you think?" One of Samuel's friends repeated the question. "What do you think happened? Why isn't she here?"

"I hear she's being shunned," Samuel admitted. "I don't know much more than that, but I hope that she does not remain shunned for long. It is not easy."

Beth hadn't expected to hear this coming from Samuel. Perhaps there was more to him than she had first thought, but she hadn't thought he was hiding something from her before. Perhaps it was simply because he thought it wasn't relevant to what was going on in their relationship.

"I'd prefer not to gossip about a friend," Beth said. "If she's been shunned, then I'm sure there's a reason she's done whatever has put her there. But what it was or why, I cannot say, and I refuse to speculate. It will do her no *gut* when she finally returns to learn that she's been gossiped about because of her actions."

She gave a scathing glare to the rest of the table before turning to Samuel.

"If this is the kind of conversation that I'll be entertaining here, I think I'm going to go check on Eli," she said. "I don't want to hear it."

With that, she picked up her plate and moved to sit with her *familye*. To her surprise, Samuel moved too. Honestly, it was to his credit. If he wouldn't tolerate that kind of gossip about someone he hardly knew, then she knew he wouldn't tolerate it at all about someone he cared about – whether it was his *kinner* later in their lives or his *fraa* if he were to remarry.

"That was not the question I asked you," he clarified. "I asked if you were all right. I don't know why they had to ask you about Leah King."

CHAPTER 10

Christmas morning finally came around, and as much as Beth had been looking forward to spending the holidays with her *sohn*, she missed the familiarity that had been established in years past. The traditions she had started with Jacob didn't quite feel as though they belonged in the *haus* her parents owned, as much as she wanted to pass them along to her *sohn*.

One of the biggest traditions she and Jacob had started after getting married was that, for Christmas morning, Beth made cinnamon rolls. They were the bakery's most popular item. Usually, she wouldn't have brought that kind of work home. Instead, just once a year for her husband, she would make the cinnamon rolls to share and enjoy.

She didn't even remember how it had *kumm* about. What Beth did know was that Eli was too young to have a cinnamon roll. Well, the kind they made at the bakery, anyway. She suspected that Eli wasn't quite ready for something so sweet, and so large.

Before she could put any more thought into it, Eli started to cry. Beth got off her bed and picked up her little one.

"It's all right, Eli," she said softly as she rocked him in her arms. "It's all right. No one's going to hurt you here."

She rocked Eli softly as he started to calm down.

"That's right. There you go," she said. "It's Christmas, Eli. *Ach,* what a time you'll have with this holiday when you're older. Right now, I suppose you're too young to truly appreciate what's going on. But we'll teach you about the reason for the holiday and the magic surrounding it. There's nothing more to hide." She smiled down at Eli, who had just snuggled into her shoulder and started to fall asleep.

Instead of waking him up, Beth started to

hum one of the Christmas hymns to him. He went limp in her arms as he fell asleep.

Once she was sure she could put him down without waking him up, she put him back on his little bed and walked out of the room. This was no place to reminisce now.

When Beth walked into the kitchen, she found that she was the first one up. That was no surprise to her. Depending on when Eli decided he wanted comfort for the morning – which usually put him right back to sleep, thankfully – she was either the first one up or the last one up. There was no in-between right now. Not with the sun starting to rise at around eight in the morning instead of six or seven.

As much as she wanted to make cinnamon rolls this year, the magic was in preparing them for baking on Christmas Eve. That allowed the dough to rise and gave her time to prepare other things while it was getting ready. Jacob always profusely thanked her when she made the cinnamon rolls.

As she started to pull out the ingredients and materials to make herself a quick breakfast, she couldn't help a glance back at the room she was sharing with Eli. As much as she found comfort in his presence, she couldn't help but wonder something else while she tried to get her mind off the way the *familye* had changed last year.

"Why does love always leave me?"

She shook her head before starting on the breakfast. That was a thought she didn't want to entertain, no matter how strongly it pulled at her head.

∽

LATER THAT DAY, Beth and Naomi sat in the living room. Their parents had left to visit their friends. According to Naomi, Isaac was visiting his parents. Beth was glad that Naomi had come to see Eli and her. It felt like many of the other people in the community somewhat skipped right over the fact that she still lived at her parents' home.

"This week has been awful, Beth. Truly awful," Naomi said as she worked on sewing a quilt that had been meant for Eli.

Naomi had never been the best at getting things finished to a strict deadline when it came to quilts and other crafts. Beth was only glad that the thought was there, and that she had been able to see the progress that her *schweschder* was making.

"What's happened, Naomi?" Beth couldn't believe that Naomi was despairing, again, but sometimes that's what it took to get the job done.

Naomi just had to be able to share her thoughts with someone and get a second opinion when she despaired like this. She was kind of surprised that Isaac hadn't already offered his thoughts on whatever was bugging her. Nonetheless, there was nothing more she could do to convince her to share with Isaac if she had decided that this was not fit for her husband to hear.

"The council rejected the bakery annex," Naomi announced pitifully. "They said something about being worried about increased foot traffic from *Englischers*. We already get plenty of *Englischers*. I don't think having the annex to fulfill orders quicker is going to impact the tranquility of the community."

"Well, the council has to act in the best interests of everyone in the community," Beth said gently. "Perhaps they've had complaints about the number of customers you get and are worried you'll get more if they give you an annex. Have you thought about revising it so that there's a way for people to be less intense about what they order?"

"Isaac's asked me to consider revising it as

well, but I don't know what I'd do about it to get it passed," Naomi admitted. "And it's bad enough that Isaac wants to see all of this through, but now that Hannah Glick's returned, I'm trying to keep my head level in so many ways."

Beth frowned a little. She didn't know what Hannah Glick had to do with any of the current events. If anything at all, she wondered if Naomi had been having trouble avoiding the excitement around her return. She'd been living in another community – if Beth understood her *mamm* correctly – and had decided to visit her *familye* for the holidays because she missed them. Was there any reason to be worried about her intentions because of that?

"Forget about Hannah Glick for now," Beth said. "Her return to the community has no bearing on what you're going to do about the bakery annex and the council."

Naomi nodded slowly, taking in a deep breath.

"I'm sorry. I suppose the bakery annex issue has been making me more sensitive to other things," her *schweschder* said as she picked up Eli to keep him from crawling out of the room. "But what am I to do about the council? It feels as though there are still some people in the community who want to see me as an outsider. I can't believe that my annex was rejected…"

"I know a lot of the older members of our community are still struggling to believe that you've truly changed, but the best way to show them that you've changed would be to consider their worries," Beth suggested. "If they're worried about the increase in *Englischer* traffic, then why don't you consider having the annex closer to where the *Englischers* usually end up coming in and out and have others staffing it?"

Naomi looked up from Eli's face to look at Beth.

"You think that would work?"

"I honestly don't know," she admitted, "but I don't see why you couldn't at least talk it over with *Daed* and Isaac. We're all rooting for this annex to go through because it's our *familye* business and the future of the *familye*. If we can't keep up with the demand that has *kumm* about because a few *Englischers* think we're one of the best bakeries they've ever eaten at, then what are we to do when we want to help the community host an event?"

"I can see the point you're making," Naomi conceded. "I don't know what else to do, though. What if that doesn't work?"

"If that doesn't work, then someone in the council is certainly being obstinate," Beth said. "But we can deal with that when we get there. For now, don't you think that it's better to focus on the fact that it's Christmas and that we're having fun with the *familye*? And the *familye* dinner? Is Isaac coming to that?"

"Isaac promised he'd be at Christmas dinner with us this year," Naomi replied. "That's part of why he felt so strongly that he had to visit his parents before dinner. I thought it would be better to send him alone and I could visit later because I wanted to hear your thoughts on the annex without him here to share more thoughts about it."

Beth nodded slowly.

"Then it sounds like I've done my job," she teased Naomi.

"How about you, Beth? What do you want out of Christmas this year?" Naomi turned an earlier question on her, and Beth was stumped.

"I... I don't know how to answer that." Beth sighed. "I really don't."

CHAPTER 11

After Naomi left to see Isaac and his *familye*, Beth went to visit a few of her friends. Others were also worried about Leah's shunning, and she wanted to know if any other interesting gossip had made the rounds. So, with Eli bundled up well, it was time to brave the cold.

"All right, Eli. Let's go!" she said as her baby squealed.

It didn't take long to get where they were going, stopping off to see Anne King first. At this time of year, not having her *dochder* at home was probably hitting a lot harder than Anne would have imagined. Beth didn't want her to feel that alone.

When she knocked on the door, Anne answered.

"*Ach*, Beth. What a pleasant surprise. And Eli!" Anne smiled. "*Kumm* in, please. It's cold out there. Warm yourselves by the fire."

"*Danke*, Anne," Beth said. "I was starting to visit people because I've been home all morning and thought that it would be best to see you first. How are you? And Leah, if you happen to know?"

Leah may not have been staying here despite the shunning, but Beth still needed to know what her friend was doing, and what in the world had possessed her to do whatever it was that got her shunned. The council didn't mess around when it came to the rules of the community and how one was supposed to conduct oneself around *Englischers*.

"I'm doing better, but Leah refuses to admit that she did anything wrong," Anne said. "She tells me the rumors have it all wrong. There's nothing inappropriate about her relationship with the *Englischer* shop owner. His horse spooked, and he didn't know how to calm it down."

"And so, she helped calm the horse?" Beth asked.

It wasn't hard to believe. Anne and Leah had

always worked with animals, as they owned a ranch in the community. She supposed that if someone needed help with animals, it would have been right to expect that Leah would help. Even if it risked her getting shunned.

"*Jah*," Anne said. "I don't think she did anything wrong either, but it's the principle to her. To punish her for being nice and helping someone… it doesn't sit well with her or me."

Beth nodded. She didn't think that it would be wise to interrupt Anne while she discussed Leah. However, she was relieved that the rumors seemed to have blown the story way out of proportion. As rumors tended to do, she supposed.

"How are you coping with Leah being shunned? I hear it's not that easy to deal with someone in your *familye* being shunned so heavily," Beth asked.

She just wanted to know how Anne was coping. She suspected that it wasn't as easy as she was attempting to make it look. If Anne was as *gut* a *mamm* as Beth suspected, Anne was torn over what to do: either to stay quiet and keep to the Ordnung decision to shun her own *dochder*, or to go to Leah and tell her that it'd be all right, eventually. A *gut mamm* would want to do both so as not to make it worse and to comfort their *kinner*.

"There are so many things I want to do, but none of them would bring about the end I'd want," Anne admitted. "Part of me wants to run and hug my *dochder* and tell her that it'll all work out eventually because she had *gut* intentions, no matter what the rumor mill is saying. Part of me wants to remain away from her and let her work it out on her own so that she learns that actions have consequences – but I think she's already learned that lesson. And there's a part of me that wants to yell at the Ordnung that she's trying to help our community instead of making us appear to be so cold to the *Englischers*."

Beth couldn't help but laugh. That sounded like Anne King. She also supposed she had options that wouldn't land her in trouble like going to see Leah would. Especially if her own *mamm* was considering the same thing.

"Well, I should be going, but I'm glad to know that you're coping," Beth said. "I don't know how long Eli will travel with me, and I want to be home while he's napping."

"And you have other people to see, I suppose," Anne replied. "Well, *danke* for stopping by. Not many other people have thought to see how I'm doing. I appreciate the thought."

Beth nodded.

With that, she lifted Eli, who had started to crawl around the *haus,* off the floor. Together, they started off toward the bishop's *haus.* She wasn't sure who else to see. As much as she knew the Ordnung was responsible for upholding the shunning, it was the bishop who had asked for the shunning. It didn't take a genius to know that if one paid attention.

Upon arriving at the bishop's home, Eli started to get fussy. She shushed him softly.

"It's all right, Eli. We're just going to make one more stop and then get you home for a nap. Perhaps I should have asked Naomi to visit while you were napping instead of first thing in the morning," she said as she knocked on the door.

It didn't take long for the bishop to answer the door and invite her and Eli in.

"Beth, it's so *gut* to see you. I didn't think you'd be out visiting with such a young *kind* this morning," the bishop said as he shut the door behind them. "What brings you here today? Is something the matter? Or just visiting because you need to get out of the *haus* and thought you might as well *kumm* to see me?"

"A little of both, actually," Beth admitted. "Bishop, I'm not sure that shunning Leah King is going to do any *gut*. You know how the rumor mill can blow things out of proportion. Have you heard her side of the story yet?"

"The *elders* and I heard her story when she was first shunned," the bishop reassured her. "I'm sorry to say that the shunning must be upheld, but there is a difference between genuinely wishing to help and wishing to help for another matter entirely. I did not believe she was entirely truthful in her motives to help this *Englischer*."

"But to shun her from her *familye* with only an inkling that she may not have been truthful with you," Beth started, "isn't that exactly the kind of behavior that we don't engage in because it gets us unfairly judged by the *Englischers*?"

"I understand your frustration with seeing one of your best friends shunned, Beth. If I didn't, I don't know that I could do my job as bishop. However, we have rules here that must be followed. If they are not followed, there are consequences. Even you know that. Your husband knew that, and while his consequences were far too much for his actions, you should understand the most out of anyone else in the community that they are needed at times."

"Jacob's death is not a consequence of trying to right the wrongs in his life," Beth said bitterly.

"I cannot end the shunning of Leah King until she repents of her actions," the bishop reaffirmed. "I'm sorry if you've *kumm* all this way to see if I would be willing to end the shunning on her without it, but there is a way of life here. If I don't enforce it, where will we be left? We'll be as lawless as the *Englischers*, and that is no way of life I mean to encourage. So, if that's all, perhaps it's time that you got going, Beth."

Seeing that the bishop wasn't going to budge on his stance and knowing that Eli was getting fussy enough that she was starting to think about putting him down early for a nap, Beth sighed. This time, she would be leaving. But she was positive that she could do more for Leah if the bishop would only listen.

"Of course. My apologies for interrupting your Christmas morning," Beth said as she stood to leave. "I'll be getting out of your hair now."

She grabbed Eli from the couch – where he was half asleep – and left the bishop's home. While he may not be ready to lift the shunning, Beth had a feeling that there was only one other option for her. She had to see Leah and hear her side. Straight from the source. It wouldn't be easy, and if the elders heard what she was doing, she could be shunned.

But wasn't extending grace to the members of the community just what the bishop prided himself on doing?

"*Ach,* Eli," she said as she trudged through the snow that had fallen the night before. "This only makes me wonder if raising you here is a *gut* idea, with all the strict, rigid rules. I don't like it. Didn't like it as a kid, and now that I'm a *mamm*, I like it even less."

She couldn't help a small laugh as Eli just let out a yawn. He didn't care. Part of her wished she could let it all roll off her back like that, too.

CHAPTER 12

Managing the bakery alone was difficult. Isaac had offered to do it during this difficult time of year for Naomi and Beth because he knew that Eli's birthday was going to be a difficult one. Beth was still trying to learn her way around life without a husband. Naomi was still somewhat afraid that Beth would not be all right and that she would have to take care of Eli. If it came to that, Isaac was more than happy to raise his nephew as his own.

But there was no point in worrying over something that had such a low likelihood.

Instead, Isaac was worried over something else entirely. He was trying to revise the annex plans to address the issues that the council had pointed out. If they were truly worried about the extra *Englischer* foot traffic that an annex would bring in, then he had to find a way to balance that out with the fact that they were struggling to keep up with demand. There were only so many ways they could do both with the bakery as it was right now.

They had already rearranged the rear of the bakery to make it more productive as far as the flow of products went. Products now came out of the oven on the furthest side of the back wall, to the table to be frosted, and then out to the customers. They desperately needed more space back there to work on more than three or four orders, depending on size.

This is what gave Isaac the idea to change the annex from spanning the entire width of the building to move it so that it extended only the back of the bakery.

Perhaps if the front of the store stayed the same, they would be able to address the worries of the council. It was a long shot, but he wondered if this would work. So, he got out a pencil and began to sketch the new design, hoping that he'd stumbled across a design that made sense.

That meant there was plenty of space for an

annex without making the council worry about the tranquility of the community.

If it was big enough, it could serve as a prep space for the dough. Then they would only have to worry about the frosting for the cinnamon rolls and for some of the sweet breads in the summer. The rear as it stood now could also function as a place to keep the orders that were waiting to be collected, instead of making customers collect from the counter.

There were options, he had discovered, and that was all that mattered to him right now. They could be shown to Naomi, who would know which would serve them best daily.

However, there was a complicating factor in everything. At the Christmas service this year, he had seen Hannah Glick for the first time since his *rumspringa*. They had decided to court while they were in the city. She had been there a year longer than he had, which is why he had her letters. He'd simply returned earlier, despite being the same age as her.

The reason she had broken it off – and what he had not yet told Naomi because he didn't know how to – was that she had decided that she wanted to remain in the *Englisch* city. She'd asked her *mamm* not to say anything to those in the community. If she was coming back now, he wondered how her life had turned out.

But he hadn't approached or asked her for one simple reason: he had seen the hurt in Naomi's eyes when she had confronted him about the letters. As much as he thought there was some avoidance going on because she withdrew when things got busy during the holiday season, Isaac had a nagging feeling that Hannah's letters had also contributed to her withdrawal this year.

How was he to tell Naomi that he had never been able to burn the letters simply because they reminded him that his life could have turned out so much worse if he had followed her to the city?

He let out a soft sigh.

"*Ach*, Naomi… I never meant to hurt you with these letters," he said as he sat the annex papers down to think on it a moment. "But you won't listen to me right now. I feel as if you need to see her leave to believe that I have no interest in her any longer."

He shook his head.

He wanted to take Naomi by the hands some days and tell her that she had nothing to worry about with him and Hannah. After all, Hannah was not the one he had made his wedding vows to. That had been Naomi. Why should she worry

NEW YEAR'S PROMISE

about Hannah, who had been in his past and for whom he now had no feelings?

Perhaps he should have thrown the letters away or burned them when he stopped courting Hannah. Whatever the case, he had kept the letters. Now, he had to deal with the consequences of that decision.

"I promise you that I will find a way to make this up to you, Naomi. I swear it," he said as he stood up from working on the annex papers.

He supposed that he could possibly have held onto the letters because his relationship with Hannah had been the model for what he wanted out of a marriage. Hannah had been one of the few women in the community with whom he had thought he'd have a happy life, originally. However, there had been one thing he hadn't been able to work with when she was around. He hadn't particularly enjoyed that she thought they needed to be stricter with their rules until she decided that rules altogether were the worst thing that had happened to her.

Isaac had always enjoyed having a little bit of wiggle room within the Ordnung. The Ordnung may not always have the clearest rules, but every rule usually had a reason behind it. If one was able to work around it and address the concerns, there would usually be a way to compromise. Usually.

The only reason for the decision not to compromise or for a chance to be denied to fix a proposal or repent of their mistakes would be when the elders regarded the true purpose to be more sinister than they were led to believe. Not many proved to be such; however, enough had for the elders to be a little more cautious when approving proposals or allowing a shunned member to return to the community.

He walked to the window, trying to shake the feelings away. Hannah had been the one to end their courtship, but the heart had funny ways of protecting itself. There was always going to be a shred of love in his heart for her. He supposed that Naomi could feel the same way about any *menner* she had courted or been seriously involved with on her *rumspringa*, but she hadn't shared any of those stories with him.

He felt it necessary to know so that he wasn't caught off-guard by the rumors about her *rumspringa* and her behavior that the community insisted on spreading – even now that she was baptized and married within the covenants of the community. He supposed that that was part of why she might have been caught off-guard.

If the community was willing to gossip so about her involvement with *Englischers* and her behavior while on her *rumspringa*, what would they say about the fact that he had kept the letters from Hannah?

He resolved right then to do something about the love letters. He had a notion to burn them. Perhaps burning one or two from the earliest stages of their writing would help him gather the courage to burn the rest of them in the fireplace. They'd make good kindling.

But the fact that Naomi had been content to improve herself within the community had drawn him to her after his relationship with Hannah. Hannah had sought whatever would feel right to her. This meant that if he had wanted to be with Hannah, he would have had to leave the community – and he could not bring himself to do that.

With Naomi, he was able to stay close to his large *familye*, and have his own eventually, without ever wondering what was going on outside the community. He also found that Naomi loved him in different ways, ways that worked better for their life than he had experienced with Hannah.

That didn't mean it didn't hurt when she

pulled away like this, but he knew that with time and patience, she would eventually reveal to him what was wrong. All he had to do was be careful and make sure that she knew he'd listen.

Being patient was easier said than done. When Naomi decided to pull away from everyone, it took a lot of coaxing to get her to share her reasons. He knew that during the last year, she had been battling the inner turmoil of trying to decide what was right: courting him or allowing him to go on to court someone else because of the rumors that would have come with courting her.

Now that they were married, he didn't care what the community had to say about her. He'd refute those rumors every time, and if she required that he show her that the letters were gone, then he'd find a way to make himself comfortable with it.

But the most important thing right now was getting this annex finished, so he sat down at the desk again and picked up the pen. He had to finish it before Naomi started to wonder what was going on, or started despairing even more about the annex.

Chapter 13

The closer the new year came, the more incensed Beth became over the bishop and the elders not allowing Leah to return. First, she had to spend Christmas alone because of the shunning. Now, she was going to have to spend the new year alone, too. It was too much for Beth to think of, but she knew that someone had to step up. That someone had to be her if no one else was going to.

She wasn't entirely sure what she was going to do, but she knew Leah needed her help.

However, she put all of that aside for a little while. The struggle between the rules and her conscience screaming that she couldn't abandon Leah in this way would just have to wait. Samuel had asked her to join him and his *kinner* for a walk today, and she didn't want to give people the chance to get the wrong idea. If she ended up shunned as well, that meant she could support Leah, but it would be horribly lonely. She knew she'd struggle even more to care for Eli than she already was if that happened, so for today, she had to placate societal expectations.

After getting dressed and ready for the walk, she went downstairs to find her *mamm*. To her surprise, she found both her parents in the living room, playing with Eli. She smiled. To see that they were happily supporting her as she tried to find a way to find some balance gave her hope for the future. However, it also meant that she was able to court and handle a job.

She wondered how her life would change if she were to marry soon as a result of a courtship starting before the new year. Would she have to stay home to take care of Eli full-time and no longer work at the bakery? Or would her husband accept her working at the bakery to bring in the extra income needed to support the child?

"Oh, you're all dressed up for the cold," Clara remarked upon seeing her as she walked out of her room. "Where are you going?"

"Samuel has asked me to accompany him and

his two *kinner* on a walk today. I think it's too cold outside for Eli to join us, unfortunately," Beth replied. "I'm not sure, but I think there's value in making this relationship work. At least allowing it to grow."

Her *mamm* nodded.

"As you should," Amos commented. "I'd hate to see you trying to raise Eli alone until he is an adult. You're a young woman. No one should have to raise a *kind* alone if it can be helped. If Samuel is more than willing to court you, then I think it would be *gut* for you. And your *mamm* and I can help you make that happen if it's what you want."

She smiled a little. While she hadn't expected her *daed* to be the one advocating for her to go out and start courting again so soon after her husband's death, she was glad that he saw that it wasn't an attempt to replace Jacob. It was an attempt to feel whole again. She'd be lying to herself if she said that she didn't feel a little incomplete without a husband.

With that, Beth left the *haus*. Samuel had asked her to meet with him at the general store. They'd walk the paths around the community from there and go their separate ways once they returned to the general store, or his *kinner* were too tired to continue. Whichever came first. She was honestly glad that he was willing to be so flexible with the plans. His *kinner* were older than Eli, but they were still at that age where even the shortest walk in the cold might be enough to tire them out or make them wish to be near a fire.

When she arrived at the general store, she found Samuel inside with his *kinner*. She smiled a little. That was probably to keep them occupied while she arrived. She felt a little bad that they had been waiting, but hopefully, they hadn't had to wait longer than a few minutes.

Samuel offered her a smile when he saw her.

"Beth! I'm so glad that you could make it," he said.

"I hope I didn't keep you waiting long," she replied. "I had to be sure that my parents would be all right watching Eli. I think it's a little too cold outside for him to be going on the long walk we have planned. He would definitely want to walk on his own, and he's not ready for that just yet."

"It's all right," Samuel commented softly. "My *kinner* were grateful for the chance to warm up in the general store before we go on a walk. They're trying to get used to the long distances because they will have to walk together eventually when they grow older. No time like the present to get them used to it."

"Indeed."

Beth smiled a little at the two *kinner* standing behind Samuel. She was sure they would recognize her from church and the community gatherings. However, she wasn't sure if they knew her name, so she leaned down to talk to them.

"My name's Beth," she said. "What are your names?"

She already knew their names, but she thought this would be a fun way to let them introduce themselves to her and let them understand that she meant them no harm.

"I'm Irene. I'm four!" The young girl giggled as she held up four fingers to indicate her age.

Beth smiled. That was always fun to see a *kind* do. She then turned to the boy, who shied against his *daed's* leg and muttered his name into Samuel's pants.

"Daniel's a bit shy," Samuel said. "I'm sure that the more time we spend together, the more he'll feel comfortable with you. It's all right, Daniel. She's just here to go on our walk with us."

With that, Daniel looked up at her. His eyes glistened a little with curiosity as he took her in. Beth was able to get a good look at Daniel and determined he was probably about six or seven. He was old enough to be in school when it started up again in the new year. Irene wasn't quite old enough yet, but next year, she certainly would be in school with her *bruder*.

"I'm six and a half," Daniel finally said in a voice that she could hear.

It was just above a whisper, but it was progress from the mumble into his *daed's* pant leg. She'd take it.

"It's a pleasure to meet you both," Beth said. "Shall we head outside then and get going on our walk?"

The two *kinner* smiled and nodded excitedly. Samuel laughed a little.

"All right then. Shall we, Beth?" He smiled at her.

She nodded and they all headed out into the cold. Thankfully, it wasn't snowing. If there had been one thing that could have possibly ruined the plans, it was snow – as far as Beth was concerned. She wasn't sure about Samuel, Irene, and Daniel's take on snow, but they all seemed fine with a walk on the snow-covered ground.

The snow had already started to melt. The sun had come out and the slowly melting snow meant the paths were more visible. She appreciated the warmth it brought to the sting of winter.

"How have you been lately, Beth?" Samuel broke the silence that had allowed Beth to start thinking.

"I've been all right. And you three?"

"We've been doing well. Daniel's excited to return to school. Never thought it would be him who was excited, but who knows how Irene will do." He smiled a little. "As long as they're happy, I'm happy. How's Eli doing? I know you left him with your parents, but I rarely see you with him."

"Oh, he's so *gut*. He's a happy *boppli*," Beth replied. "I wish I could carry him everywhere still. Now that he's learning how to walk, he's harder to take places."

Samuel laughed a little at this comment. She supposed he would have gone through the same with both Irene and Daniel. She appreciated that the laugh was light-hearted and happy, not what she had expected from someone who had already done his time with that stage of parenting.

"It can be a difficult age, but parenting only gets more rewarding the older the *kinner* get," Samuel said. "I know that I've had a *gut* many rewarding moments with mine."

Beth nodded slowly.

The more he opened to her, the more she wondered why he had remained a widower after the death of his *fraa*. He was one of those *menner* who had every quality someone would have been looking for. Perhaps it was because he had *kinner* that he had not courted again.

Beth, however, was slowly starting to wonder if there was any reason that she shouldn't be courting Samuel.

CHAPTER 14

Naomi had decided that she was going to investigate why the annex for the bakery had been rejected. She needed to know, even if that reason was never shared with anyone besides her. Had there been an influence on the decision, she wanted a chance to defend herself or Isaac – or even the rest of her *familye* – against the accusations before they became fodder for the gossip mills.

So, she decided to talk to an old friend of hers whose *daed* was an elder. She would probably know since the elders tended to share their decisions with their families first, and then with the ones who would be affected by said decisions.

While Naomi didn't know the reasons, it gave her a *gut* idea of who to talk to and who to question.

When she arrived at the *haus*, she found her friend – a woman named Esther – at the dining room table.

"Naomi! What a pleasure to see you again," Esther said. "I've not been able to see you since you got married. How is married life treating you? How's Isaac?"

"Married life is treating me well, and Isaac's doing well," Naomi replied as she pulled her cloak off. "There's nothing I like more than coming to see friends, so I'm glad that you were willing to meet with me."

The two spent some time catching up on each other's lives over a cup of coffee before Naomi ventured to divulge her reason for being there.

"Do you mind if I ask you what you've heard your *daed* say about the bakery annex? I need to know the reasons behind the concerns about the *Englischer* foot traffic and its impact on the tranquility of the community."

Esther set her cup of coffee down at the table and furrowed her brow.

"I didn't think you'd be one to question the reasons behind the elders' decisions," she said softly. "Is everything all right, Naomi? Are you sure that you're doing all right?"

"I'm sure," Naomi reassured Esther. "I'm still a popular topic in the gossip mill, and I wanted to hear from someone in the know before the rumors reach me. You understand, *jah*?"

Esther nodded slowly.

"Well, Naomi, I'm not sure you're going to like the answer. Are you still sure you want to know?"

Esther appeared to be attempting to pad whatever she was going to say. While Naomi appreciated that her friend was trying to protect her feelings, there was enough of that going on in the community. She didn't need her feelings protected when she was quite capable of doing that or defending herself.

"I can handle it, Esther."

Her friend let out a soft sigh before thinking about the best way to say what she needed to say. This worried Naomi. If she had to think about what she was going to say, then there were only a couple of things that could have had any impact on what had happened with the elders' decision to say that they were worried about increased *Englischer* foot traffic. And it wasn't the fact that a few *Englischers* had decided to post online that they really liked the food available at the bakery.

"Your past mistakes did have some sway on that decision," Esther finally said. "While you've been back in the community for a good few years, there's always been a worry in the back of the elders' minds. You got involved with the party scene, Naomi. No one who's gotten involved with the party scene on their *rumspringa* has decided to stay this long."

Hearing that, Naomi's knees felt as though they would have buckled if she wasn't sitting down already. She looked at Esther.

"Are you sure?" She didn't want to believe that was the reason, but she had asked Esther for the truth.

If that was the truth, she had some serious thinking to do about whether she was considered to be a part of the community or not now that she had repented. What could the elders have to worry about now that she was home and sober, especially after her marriage? She was even incredibly specific about ensuring that alcohol was never an ingredient in the products turned out by the bakery.

She didn't want to go back down that path. How could the elders believe that she would throw away all that she had finally gained now that she was happy to have a *gut* life?

"I asked you if you were sure you wanted to know, Naomi," Esther reminded her. "There's no reason for you to think that you're going to win over everyone. The older community members, especially, have a hard time believing that anyone has truly repented. That's partly why the rules of the Ordnung are so strict. You have to be willing to risk it all to sin, and if you're willing to risk it all, they're not going to believe that you're going to give it all up again to return."

"Then why even offer repentance at that point?" Naomi asked, confused.

Would they have accepted that same behavior for themselves? Or were they so strict with everyone else because they had made mistakes, almost lost everything, and didn't want anyone else to repeat those mistakes while they were able to apply the rules?

"I don't know," Esther said. "However, I do know that the council is worried that once *Englischers* learn that you were once among their party scene, the wrong crowd is going to *kumm* to the bakery. I don't know how you're going to convince anyone otherwise, because I tried to convince them that you were no longer that careless young woman. I couldn't get them to listen to me."

Naomi let out a heavy sigh.

"*Danke,* anyway, Esther." She stood up. "I should probably be going, then. That was all I needed."

Esther nodded as if she understood that there was more on her mind than just the matter of the annex.

As Naomi walked out of Esther's home, she couldn't help but be reminded of all her problems besides having to convince the elders that her bakery annex wouldn't attract the wrong crowd. Hannah Glick had returned for the holidays, but she had made no move to talk to Isaac. Either that or Isaac was avoiding her in an attempt to alleviate Naomi's concerns. Whatever the truth might be, she did know that she felt more stress than was necessary during the holiday season because of Hannah's presence and the annex being rejected.

It didn't help that Eli was to turn one in a few days. That itself was a traumatic date that she didn't entirely want to remember. She never wanted to have to relive the experience of finding Beth in a pool of blood as she had a year ago, and nor did she want to be reminded of it.

While she walked home, she pulled the cloak closer around her body. How could all of this be

NEW YEAR'S PROMISE

happening during what was supposed to be the greatest, happiest time of year? She could understand that Beth and the trauma of Eli's birth hadn't been planned. As for the rest, however, she could not help but feel as though the universe was trying to tell her that she wasn't going to get out of having hardships any time soon. It did not matter that all she wanted at this point was a couple of weeks around the holidays during which she didn't have to worry about any of this.

Upon arriving home, she found Isaac at the fireplace in the living room. He held something in his hands, muttering as if he was reading over it to himself. The box of letters was nowhere in sight. That, at least, was something to celebrate right now. With Hannah's reappearance, she was not going to take any chances. That box of letters needed to go.

"*Ach*. Naomi. I almost didn't hear you walk in," Isaac said as he looked up from what he was doing. "How was your talk with Esther?"

"Informative," Naomi snapped.

She kept her answers short and clipped as Isaac tried to pull the information out of her. She didn't want to talk to anyone right now. As much as she wanted to tell him that, something inside her prevented her from doing so. As soon as Isaac realized that he wasn't going to get much out of her, he left her to retreat into their bedroom to pull away from everyone.

In the privacy of the bedroom, Naomi took off her cloak and kicked off her boots. She pulled the covers back on the bed before crawling under them and burying her face in the pillow. Instead of using the time that Isaac was allowing her to pull away productively to settle her emotions, she let the tears run free. Part of her knew this was going to help her regulate her emotions so much more than anything else she could do.

She just wanted the rest of the world to leave her alone for the holidays so that she could at least enjoy the new year's activities without having to worry about the future of the bakery or her marriage.

CHAPTER 15

Beth took in a deep breath. Her parents were going to be watching Eli, but not for the reasons they thought. She had told them they were going to be watching Eli because she needed to run some errands. While what she was doing could indeed be counted as an errand, it wasn't the kind of errand she wanted them to know about. Yet.

She was going to see Leah. Despite knowing that her friend was shunned, she didn't want to let this shunning stand. Not without doing what she could to support her friend. With the way the rumor mill worked, she was surprised Leah hadn't yet been completely kicked out of the community with nowhere to go. She supposed it was a testament to the bishop's will that Leah still had a place to call home for now.

Perhaps her conversation with the bishop had some impact after all. That would have made Beth's day.

As she walked along the paths in the community, Beth couldn't help but wonder what she was supposed to do. If no one would take Leah at her word that she had only stopped to help the *Englischer* with his horse, would they believe she could repent? Or would Leah go through the same ordeals as Naomi had after her *rumspringa*?

Beth shook her head. This was not the time to be thinking about how it all could end. If anything, this was the time to be thinking about how great it would be to have Leah as a full member of the community again. After all, that was her goal.

Upon arriving at Leah's *haus*, Beth knocked. This was perhaps the riskiest part of her plan. If anyone caught her here, they would have to ask what she was doing. While the answer in theory would get support, she knew that in practice, it was almost asking for the community to shun her as well. Her only hope was that Leah would appreciate the visit more than she would fear the consequences of Beth coming to visit.

When the door opened, Beth smiled. Leah

NEW YEAR'S PROMISE

stood before her, dressed as if she had not been shunned by the community. It probably helped to keep her spirits up that her shunning would be properly ended despite showing no remorse for helping the *Englischer*.

"What are you doing here, Beth?" Leah spoke in almost a whisper. "Don't you know that the rumor mill is a cruel piece of this community?"

"Then let me in, Leah," Beth replied. "I can leave from the back door, if you like, but please. I needed to see you and hear your side of the story."

Leah relented after thinking about it for a moment. With Beth inside, Leah closed the door as quickly as she could – almost as if she was looking out for Beth's well-being in the community. Beth appreciated this, but there was no need to worry about her own reputation in the community.

"Is there anything more to the story than trying to help the *Englischer* store owner settle his horse?" Beth asked, knowing her time here was short.

Leah shook her head.

"*Nee*. I just helped him settle his horse. He gave my hand a squeeze for the trouble. Other than that, I don't see any reason for the elders and the bishop to have gotten up in a fuss like this," she replied. "Why are you really here, Beth? We both know that you wouldn't be risking your standing in the community if you weren't searching for more."

"I've been thinking about how strictly to raise Eli," Beth admitted, "and the more I see the community treat you so harshly for a simple act of kindness, the more I'm worried that I don't want him being exposed to such a strict Ordnung."

Leah let out a soft laugh.

"*Ach*, Beth. You always had a *gut* heart," her friend said. "I don't doubt for a minute that you'll be able to raise Eli with the right kind of rules – whatever you deem the right ones to be. But you should really be going. I don't want you getting into trouble, too… as much as I appreciate the visit."

With a soft smile from Leah, Beth left through the back door. It led more towards the center of the community, and once she was far enough away, she could say that she had come from home. With a soft wave, Beth started in the direction of the general store.

Knowing that Leah was not denying her actions was helpful. However, there was only so much Leah could do about her shunning if she didn't acknowledge the repentance the community was looking for.

Once she was far enough away from Leah's *haus* not to have to worry about being found out, Beth slowed down. In fact, now that she had spoken to her friend, she found that she wasn't nearly as worried about raising Eli. Perhaps it was because she was questioning how she had grown up.

Could it be possible that spiritual questioning, in a way, showed conviction because it meant that one had decided to stay with the religion despite all the obstacles that one had faced? Both Beth and Leah appeared to have done just this. She wondered if that had anything to do with the fact that Leah had been shunned, and Naomi had been struggling with the community's disdain.

"Beth!"

A voice startled her out of her thoughts. She stopped in her tracks and looked around. Instead of finding the bishop – which was her worst fear– she found herself face to face with Samuel. His *kinner* were nowhere to be found, and she assumed that he had left them in the care of someone. She didn't mind encountering him alone since they would have a chance to talk without having to watch what they said, unlike

GRACE LEWIS

when they were on the walk with Irene and Daniel.

"*Hallo*, Samuel," she replied. "What brings you out this way?"

"*Ach*, just heading to the general store for some flour," he said. "And you?"

"For sugar." She offered a smile. "You can never have enough sugar."

He nodded.

"Would you like to walk together? The general store isn't that much further, and I could walk you home after we finish shopping."

His words made the entire world stop right there. He wanted to walk her home. That was almost always a tell-tale sign of a man wishing to court a young woman. Walking her home… and he wanted to walk Beth home. She wasn't sure she was ready to open her heart just yet, but she couldn't deny that it would be a *gut* way to hide that she had been at Leah's home.

After all, they did need sugar.

"We can at least walk to the general store together," Beth finally said. "I'm not quite sure how I feel about the rest."

He nodded slowly.

"Fair enough. Shall we, then?"

With that, they set off in the direction of the

general store. Neither spoke during the walk. She wondered if he wasn't sure what else to say. She had turned down perhaps the first step in a courtship, for now.

"Do you think you're ready for another courtship?" Samuel broke the silence. Beth hadn't expected him to want to know the answer, and if she were honest with herself, she wasn't sure she knew the answer. She pursed her lips. At the least, he deserved some kind of answer.

"I'm not sure," she replied, heaving a soft sigh. "There's been so much going on in my life that a courtship has been the furthest thing from my mind."

"That's an understandable answer. I was like that for quite some time after my *fraa* passed away," Samuel revealed. "But lately, I have felt that I am perhaps ready to court again. More specifically, I feel the desire to court you, Beth."

The heat on her cheeks told her what she already knew. There was a blush spreading rapidly, and there was no use denying that it was nice to feel wanted by him. By anyone in the community, even. She'd worried that because she had a *boppli*, no one in the community would be willing to court her. To have a *kind* while courting was usually unheard of, but it could happen when spouses passed on early in life.

They arrived at the general store, which was enough for Beth to shake these thoughts away. Except for one.

"If you were to court me, how would you treat me?" Beth decided to ask the question because she had some concerns.

Jacob had been able to hide some of the worst of his behavior until they had been married. She didn't want to go through something like that again.

"I would treat you properly," he said with conviction. "You've already been through so much that I want to take your stress away. I'm not sure how much stress I could feasibly remove from your life, given I'd be adding two more *kinner* to it, but I hope you'd at least give me a chance."

They walked into the general store and the conversation stalled while they got their supplies. Beth hefted the bag of sugar up into her arms into a more comfortable position so that she could carry it more easily. Samuel carried his bag of flour in one hand.

"I suppose it has been long enough that the best way to know for sure if I'm ready is to try,"

Beth said tentatively as they exited the shop. "Would you still like to escort me home?"

Samuel grinned widely.

"Beth Fisher, it'd be my honor to escort you home from the general store today," he said.

With that, they started towards her parents' home.

CHAPTER 16

After dropping the sugar off at home and making sure that Sam wouldn't be around to question where she was going next, Beth left the *haus*. Her parents had taken Eli out for a walk or out to visit more members of the community, which normally would have made her angry. However, because it meant they weren't around to see her come home and immediately leave again, she wasn't all that upset about it today. Besides, Eli was almost a year old and deserved to visit and get to know others in the community.

Her next stop was the bishop's *haus*. She had to at least attempt one more time to make sure that he would reinstate Leah. If she didn't, she felt as though she was failing her friend. Leah had been one of her best supports during her year alone with Eli.

The walk to the bishop's *haus* didn't take all that long. He didn't live far from her parents, which made it both easy and more nerve-wracking.

She knocked at the door, hoping that he was home. If he wasn't, she wasn't sure when she might have an opportunity to speak to him. As the bishop, he would have had plenty of responsibilities that took him away from home.

The door opened, and to her delight, she was faced with the bishop. She smiled at him.

"Beth. Please, *kumm* in," he *invited* as he moved aside so that she could walk in. "I wasn't expecting company, but I'm now intrigued. What's brought you all the way here?"

"I'd like you to reinstate Leah," Beth said confidently.

"We've already had this conversation, Beth," the bishop said patiently. "She's helped an *Englischer* and she shows no remorse for it."

"The *Englischer* is an older *mann*," Beth explained. "Please. At least hear out the rest of the story before you decide that only her repentance is *gut* enough to reinstate her. I promise you that I wouldn't have *kumm* here if I didn't believe that there was a reason for you to do this."

The bishop looked at her with pursed lips before letting out a sigh.

"You have ten minutes, Beth," he relented. "If you cannot convince me in ten minutes, I do not want to hear another word on this subject from you. Do you understand me?"

Beth nodded.

It wasn't ideal, but it would have to do. She took in a deep breath. If she only had ten minutes, every word counted.

"Leah told me the story," she started. "She helped an *Englischer,* sure, but the *Englischer* squeezed her hand to thank her for the help. I remember plenty of older *Englischer menner* doing the same to me on my *rumspringa.*" She took in a deep breath, trying to gauge where the bishop's thoughts were going. "Besides, spiritual conviction is one of the main reasons we live this way, is it not?"

"You are right about spiritual conviction, but I do not see how that has anything to do with Leah's decision to help," the bishop said. "Please enlighten me."

That was exactly what Beth wanted to hear.

"She was questioning the policy of not helping

Englischers unless absolutely necessary because she wanted to see what kind of reaction she'd get in herself," Beth explained. "We've all had moments like that, I believe, where we just want to see if we're doing the right thing by following this religion. Even after we've been baptized. She questioned the traditions out of conviction, Bishop."

"I see..." The bishop sat down on one of the couches, thinking about what he wanted to do.

It certainly wasn't an easy decision, and Beth was going to let him think as long as he needed. She had said all she needed to, and she hoped it was enough at this point.

"You have supported a friend despite what it could cost you," the bishop started. "That's certainly worthy of praise, Beth. You have grace and wisdom beyond your years and it is my hope that the rest of the community can learn from you. I will have the elders reinstate her immediately. Leah King has conviction unlike anyone else in this community, and I'll admit that I was baffled she would behave in this way without thinking about the consequences first."

Beth smiled widely.

That was more than enough for her.

"*Danke,* Bishop," she said. "That's all I needed to hear."

"I should be thanking you, Beth." He stood up at this point. "If it wasn't for grace and wisdom, I don't know where this community would be. *Danke* for reminding me that sometimes all we can rely on is the grace of others to get where we need to be."

Naomi looked over the revised annex plan that Isaac had drawn up. He had been paying a lot more attention to her lately, and she wasn't sure how she felt about that. It was what she had wished for after she had found the letters, but not like this. He was paying more attention to how they were going to secure the *familye* future. She supposed she should have been thanking him for that. After all, her original annex plan had been rejected.

If it wasn't for Isaac, she wasn't sure that she would be able to write a plan that would be approved. If the council was honestly that worried about increased *Englischer* foot traffic, then they would have to take it up with the blogs that were posting more about the food and the atmosphere than Naomi and Isaac.

She put the revised plans down. They were *gut*. The plans mentioned some of the other worries that Naomi had not been able to properly express, no matter how much she had tried. Isaac had thought to include the adaption of another exit so that they could properly funnel people in and out instead of having a line out the door that made it hard for people to *kumm* in and out.

They would come in one door, queue up for their orders, and then exit through the other door. There would, of course, still be tables and chairs and places for people to gather and enjoy their purchases inside. However, the separate entrance and exit would help with the traffic. If that didn't cut down on the *Englischers* disrupting the peace, she wasn't sure what would by the council's standards.

"*Hallo.*"

Isaac's voice brought her out of her thoughts. She looked up to find him standing in the doorway between the living room and the dining room.

"Hi, Isaac," she said with a soft smile. "I appreciate the work you've done on revising the bakery annex plans. I think that enlarging the rear so that we can keep up with orders, as well as your other changes, will be the answers the council is seeking. They're *gut* ideas to deal with the crowds, too."

He smiled.

"I'm glad that you like the plans," he said. "I wasn't sure what else to add. Do you think there's anything else we could or should add that would impress the council? Or at least make them more likely to listen?"

"I think it should be you presenting the new plan to them," Naomi said. "Isaac, someone decided that because I messed up big time on my *rumspringa,* we're seeing all the *Englischer* foot traffic. I beg to differ, but I don't think they'll listen to me."

Isaac put his arms around her, hugging her tightly for a few brief seconds before he pulled away. She looked up at his face. She couldn't entirely read his thoughts by the expression on his face, but she hoped that he was going to say something that would make her feel less like this was her fault.

"If the council refuses to see that this is what needs to happen because they're too hung up on the mistakes you've repented of, then that is their problem. Not yours," Isaac said, enunciating each word so that she had no choice but to hear each one individually. "Besides, you have one of the few hearts in the community that does *gut* to do *gut*. You don't care how it makes you look to the community. Just as it ought to be."

This made her blush quite deeply. Although Isaac was her husband, and thus should be complimenting her in a way that would cause her to blush, she was having a hard time believing this one. If it was true, why would the elders continue to see her as the woman who did wrong and partook in drugs during her *rumspringa*? As if she was nothing more than the woman who had dated an *Englischer* who hadn't converted.

"That shade of red on your cheeks is exactly what I hoped to see," he continued. "You will be able to have anything you want if you are able to shake off the judgmental elders. If you still feel that I should be the one to present to the council, then I will, but make that decision closer to when we present the revised plan. All right?"

Naomi nodded.

This conversation, and the entire conversation around the annex, had reminded her that she could determine her destiny going forward. And she was determined to do so, reconnecting with the strength and courage needed.

CHAPTER 17

New Year's Eve came around and Naomi felt more at peace with the way her life had turned out. She may not have been the best example of how to stay on the path the community put forward as the best way to live one's life, but she thought herself a good example of how to return to the path. She had done it once before. If needed, she could absolutely do it again if the elders decided she was behaving in an unadvised way. It wouldn't be easy, but when was repentance ever easy?

Today, she had decided to take a walk around the community. It had snowed during the night, so there was fresh snow pretty much everywhere. It looked so peaceful. After the turmoil that had come around this Christmas season, she was glad for the peacefulness of the snow. It was the season for new beginnings, after all.

She started humming as she walked.

"Oh, *hallo*. Wait, don't go."

The voice pulled her out of her thoughts. Naomi looked around but saw no one. The voice sounded as though it was coming from further up the path. Carefully, and quietly, she started walking through the snow.

"Wait! I only mean to apologize!"

The voice was getting louder, and it was that of a female. She heard mutterings that indicated a second person, but she couldn't decipher a second identity by the muttering she heard. And it was already a feat that she hadn't recognized the first voice.

Rounding a corner, she found herself close enough to recognize Isaac and Hannah Glick. Hannah was facing her, with Isaac facing the forest. It took her a moment to register what she was seeing, but undeniably, Hannah was kissing Isaac.

"Hannah." Isaac managed to give something of a stern warning, which made Hannah pull away.

How could he?

Naomi ran away from the scene, tears in her

eyes. She didn't want to hear any of the reasons he might try to give her. He'd told her it was all over between the two of them, and here he was, kissing her! How could he betray the vows he had made to her on their wedding day by doing that?

Upon arriving at a clearing in the woods, Naomi sank to her knees in the snow, letting her tears run freely down her face.

"I knew I should have burned those letters!"

She said this to no one in particular, as she was positive that she was alone in the woods. Covering her face with her hands, Naomi curled in on herself. Her shoulders hunched forward. The sobs rang out around her as if she was the only person for miles. And Naomi wanted nothing more than that right now.

When her tears finally stilled, she looked up from her hands which were frozen. She balled her fingers into a fist to get the circulation going again. Perhaps it would have been best to head home instead of sobbing her heart out in the forest.

"Naomi!"

Isaac's voice pierced her ears.

He was the last person she wanted to speak to. She gulped hard. If he heard her, he was going to try to explain what she had happened upon.

There was nothing to explain, though. She'd clearly seen him kissing Hannah Glick, despite all his reassurances that there was no reason for her to be worried about their relationship.

She stood up slowly.

Crack!

"That... that didn't sound *gut*..."

Naomi slowly waddled backward, only to find that her footing was no longer stable. She let out a scream as she plunged to the ground, expecting to hit the ice that had cracked underneath her. Except, her back was now wet...

And water filled her nose and mouth as she disappeared beneath the surface of the lake. Because of the fresh snow, she had inadvertently wandered onto the frozen lake. With her weight distributed on her knees and hands, the ice hadn't cared to crack and held her weight. The moment she stood up, she sealed her fate.

She managed to get her head above the water, sputtering. But the cold water and her already icy hands made it a struggle to move or attempt effectively to get herself out.

And her woolen clothing only dragged her back under. She kicked hard to get back up to the surface, hoping she'd be able to get out despite the struggle it proved to be.

"Naomi!"

She heard Isaac's muffled voice and instinctively called out to him, but regretted it the moment the cold water hit her lungs. Struggling against the water, Naomi attempted once again to get above the water. She barely succeeded, and now her arms and face were freezing as she breached.

"Isaac!"

Somewhere, amidst the depths of this experience, she found the strength to yell his name.

Her eyes were heavy as she tried not to succumb to submerging once again beneath the icy surface of the water.

She swore she heard her name being called once more before her lungs took in water instead of the fresh air she so desperately needed. In her panic, she missed the feeling of arms around her waist.

It only took a moment before her face was above the water. Naomi let out a loud, hacking cough as she tried to rid her lungs of the icy water. She felt a pair of hands on her shoulders. Once she could freely breathe again, she looked up to see who had pulled her out of the water.

There, she saw Isaac's worried eyes.

"Are you all right, Naomi?"

She nodded slowly. He helped her up, pulling her close against him despite her soaked clothing.

"Let's get you home and out of those clothes. Get you warm. Maybe get some soup in you," he continued as he started walking her home. "What were you doing out here, anyway?"

"W-Walking," Naomi managed to stutter.

She didn't want him to know that she had seen him kiss Hannah. Not yet. If he knew that, what would he think of her? Would he think that she was more dramatic than needed, or would he understand that seeing him kiss her had sent every insecurity she had into overdrive?

Considering he didn't have many insecurities in the first place, she didn't think that he would have understood how jealous she had felt since seeing the letters.

"Well, I think you should walk on home with me," he said, attempting to make a joke so that he could lighten the mood.

It worked to the extent that Naomi managed a half-laugh, which immediately turned into a cough. More water came out as she coughed. She wondered what would have happened if Isaac hadn't jumped in after her.

That was when she realized why he hadn't cared that her clothing was soaked and that she was frozen to the touch. He was, too. She could feel the water from her cloak and his shirt dripping into the snow at their feet. Perhaps she was lucky, after all, that he had seen her go missing.

"*Danke*," she said softly as they walked.

"Naomi, I'll always be there when you're in trouble," he reminded her. "I made a vow to you. There's nothing in the world that could change that."

His voice was remarkably firm, belying the fact that he had just plunged into the ice water to save her. And that he had just kissed the woman who had left him to seek a bigger life in the *Englischer* city or another Amish community. She didn't know why Hannah was here, and she honestly didn't care. Not after her lucky escape from the icy water, anyway.

They arrived home shortly after, and Naomi walked into the bedroom where, with Isaac's help, she stripped off her wet clothing. After drying off and putting on some warm, dry clothes, she sat in front of the fire that Isaac had made. When she was warm, he went to dry off and put on dry clothes. She huddled beneath a blanket on the couch and put another around her shoulders. Her body shook incessantly, she supposed as an aftereffect of having taken a plunge in the icy waters.

She wanted nothing more to do with the cold today.

Sitting in front of the fire, Naomi contemplated what she had seen in the forest that had led to her ending up in the lake. What she had seen was simply Hannah and Isaac kissing. She supposed there were plenty of ways that could have come about, but none of them satisfied her need to know what had truly happened. Part of her wanted to ask him over dinner how he had come to be kissing her, but she wondered if that would be a good idea.

After all, if he didn't want her to know, there was a good possibility this could lead to an argument. She didn't want to fight with him after what had just happened. It was almost too beautiful a moment for her to mess it up. Besides, they were both shivering, freezing messes. Any conversation to be had right now was probably best kept short.

The explanation of Hannah and Isaac kissing would not be a short one. She could almost guarantee that.

Isaac emerged, dry and clothed, and sat beside her in front of the fire. She didn't share the quilt, but he had come prepared. Perhaps because she had been submerged longer, or because he knew she was prone to getting cold more easily, he had come out with his own blanket.

"I'll make some soup after my hands stop shaking," Isaac said softly. "I'm just glad you're safe. You're all right. I'd at least let the physician look you over tomorrow. Never know what could happen after you find yourself under the water in a lake like that."

Naomi nodded.

"I'll go see him tomorrow, then," she said.

He hugged her softly and pressed a kiss to her cheek. Naomi almost froze there in his arms. Why would he kiss her after the way he had acted around Hannah this morning?

CHAPTER 18

New Year's Eve finally came around. Naomi was ready to let the year fall away as forgotten memories, especially after the way the holiday season had turned out. However, another miracle had taken place this year. Last year, Beth recovering from her traumatic birth as well as she did was considered a miracle in her *familye*. Though this one was less public, Naomi considered it a miracle all the same: having Isaac help her out of the frozen lake taught her that he was willing to risk all that he cared about – down to his own life – to make sure that she was okay.

After everything they had been going through with the letters and her hidden jealousy, it had been a welcome realization.

Over the last few days, Naomi had been far less jealous. They hadn't seen Hannah Glick again, but she supposed that was partially because Hannah hadn't been planning to stay all that long. She wondered if Hannah had been called away by other, more important matters. Whatever the reason, she was glad to know that Isaac wouldn't have to worry about how she would react to seeing him celebrate the new year with Hannah around.

Today, she was quilting beside a small fire in the living room. She had promised Beth she would make this quilt and she was determined to finish it. Naomi didn't care how long it took her. Eli deserved this one quilt made by his aunt, even if it took far longer to finish than she had originally thought it would. When he got older, she hoped he would understand the sacrifices it took to make it – even if most women in the community could have finished it before he was born.

"Naomi, what are you thinking of making for dinner tonight?"

Isaac's voice rang out through the *haus*. She smiled a little as she pinned her needle through the fabric. For the last couple of days, it had been business as usual in their home. She appreciated this more than he would ever know, if only because she had been able to let go of much of the jealousy.

"I was thinking a potato stew," she replied as he walked into the living room, carrying more wood to store inside for their fireplace. "Do you need help with the wood?"

"*Nee.* But here's something I've noticed in the last few days," he said as he put the wood down. "You've been far more chipper lately than you were before the holiday season. What's happened to make this change?"

He turned to look at her. Naomi pressed her lips together, not entirely sure how she wanted to answer that. It didn't end up mattering, though.

"Ever since you found the letters from Hannah, you've been distant with me," he continued. "What's going on, Naomi? You can't hide like this forever. Eventually, you have to share what's made you so mad. What's made you pull away from me like this?"

He walked to meet her on the couch and put a hand on her cheek.

"You're what matters the most in my life," he finished. "Let me help you with what is going on. With the feelings that you're not sure how to process, or the feelings that you don't think it would be graceful to admit to. How do you ever plan to learn how to deal with them if you cannot even admit that you have to feel them first?"

She laughed a little, but only because he was right. There was so much she wanted to do that it was hard to pinpoint the right way to deal with these feelings. However, she had a feeling that he had finally noticed how she was feeling because she had been more intimate with him lately. Not a lot more, but enough that it was clear that she had been struggling with her feelings earlier.

"Well... when I found those letters originally, the first emotion that came to me was jealousy," Naomi started. "It was entirely irrational, I know. You made your wedding vows to me. Not to Hannah Glick. But I still couldn't help but wonder if you had kept those letters from her, what was stopping you from still having feelings for her that you couldn't act on because she left the community?"

"Naomi..." Isaac started to speak but found that his words failed him.

Naomi didn't feel a need to continue speaking quite yet. The look on Isaac's face told her that he had never considered the letters could have made her feel jealous of Hannah and the way he kept her connected to his life.

"And when you kissed her in the forest, I was

afraid my worst fears had come true," she finally continued, her voice struggling to stay even. "I know that I had no reason to think that you would ever do that with her, but when I saw you kiss her... I didn't know what I was going to do. I ran. Ended up in the lake, and... and you know how that ended."

Isaac didn't say a thing, he just took her hands and squeezed them tightly. She wondered why he was doing this, but she supposed it was his way of saying that he was sorry he hadn't been able to pick up on these emotions.

"On top of it all, I worried that you would have trouble being intimate with me," she continued. "You didn't tell me that you still had letters from an old flame and left me to find them on my own while I was unpacking. If you could do that, what else had you hidden from me that would affect our relationship that I hadn't learned in a year of marriage?"

"Naomi, I never meant to hurt you," he said as he knelt beside her on the floor. "I didn't know what to tell you about the letters because I had almost completely forgotten that I had them in there, to be honest. I meant to empty that box before we moved into this *haus*." He moved tendrils of her hair out of her face.

"Do you have any other secrets you're hiding? Please, tell me now if so," she said softly. "I can't do this again, Isaac. You've made vows to me, vows that should be honored as they are just as important as the rest of what we do as a married couple. If you have any other secrets that I should know, I want to know before they are inadvertently forced on me one at a time."

He laughed a little. Although she normally wouldn't appreciate a laugh at a time like this, this one was different. It appeared to be a laugh of confidence.

"That's the only thing I was hiding, and it wasn't even deliberate," he said, attempting to soothe her fears. "Can you forgive me for putting you through that? I never meant to hurt you, and if I had remembered I had those hidden away in the closet, I would have taken care of them myself."

Naomi smiled a little.

"I can forgive you, Isaac," she said, putting her hand on top of his. "I'll focus on our future instead of the past now. There's little we can do about what happened in our past. But we can make sure our futures are bright and that we are ready for any eventuality."

Isaac nodded slowly before pressing a kiss to her forehead.

"You're an amazing woman, Naomi. I'm so very lucky to have married you," he said. "I don't know that anyone else would have forgiven me for the letters. That would make for a very difficult marriage, not being able to forgive your spouse for a clear misunderstanding."

"What do you call the kiss then?" Naomi asked, curious.

She wasn't mad about it now that he had shared that he had meant to get rid of the letters and had just forgotten to. Perhaps it was difficult to do, emotionally, because he had once been so emotionally connected to Hannah. She held onto a quilt that was about ready to fall apart for the same reason. At one point, she was sure those letters had meant the world to Isaac.

"It was a misunderstanding," Isaac clarified. "We had been talking about what happened, and she was apologizing for ripping my heart out. I wanted to end the conversation because she had insisted that we do it in the woods where we could be alone. I was afraid that the setting might lead to something like this, where you saw us and misunderstood what we were doing. She kissed my cheek as a final goodbye.

I turned to wish her goodbye, and our lips happened to meet. I froze. So did she. There was no kiss, really. Not as you and I would have kissed, at least."

Naomi nodded slowly. She could handle that version of events. If he was lying to save his marriage, she was not mad about it. Instead, she was appreciative that he understood there were certain ways to make sure an argument ended.

"Now, I don't know about you, but I'm hungry," Naomi said. "Perhaps I should get started on that potato stew I mentioned earlier."

Isaac nodded.

"We're all *gut?*" he asked as they got up from the couch.

"The letters are forgiven, and so is the accidental kiss," Naomi replied. "I don't see any reason to hold either one of those against you now that I know that you've struggled with it as much as I did. We don't deserve to be stuck in a marriage where we're both unhappy but cannot get out of it."

He nodded slowly.

"Then, potato stew sounds great, Naomi." With that, he went to put another log on the fire.

Naomi walked into the kitchen. Feeling much lighter in her heart, she started to pull the ingredients and pot out to make potato stew. She decided their future looked quite bright. If nothing else, she was sure that Isaac was the *mann* for her. The way he had soothed her worries only reminded her of why she had fallen in love with him in the first place.

CHAPTER 19

New Year's Day came, and Beth found herself quite excited. Leah had been reinstated, and her entire *familye* was going to celebrate. After they had heard Leah's side of the story from the horse's mouth, so to say, her parents had been angry that the bishop had ever thought that shunning was the right way to approach the situation. The elders could be held accountable for upholding the inappropriate punishment, but it had been the bishop who had ordered the shunning originally.

The punishment absolutely did not fit the actions. Besides, Leah's spiritual questioning showed conviction the likes of which the community had not seen in anyone since the bishop had started asking around about how to better help the people. It was simply a circumstance in which misinformation had exacerbated the situation.

"Are you excited to see that Leah will be reinstated, Beth?" Clara asked as they got themselves ready for the day.

"*Jah, Mamm*," Beth replied. "Leah is one of my closest friends. The fact that my talking to the bishop played a part in her resuming a *gut* standing within the community is just kind of the cherry on the top, as the *Englischers* may say."

Clara smiled. There was always time for a sweet smile, and Clara's in particular was among the sweetest in the community. It helped that there was no one else in the room right now. Her *daed* was taking care of Eli and getting him ready to visit the King *familye*. Meanwhile, Beth and Clara were doing their hair.

They had washed it the night before, and the braids hadn't stayed in very well. It left Beth with quite a lot of time to kill, though.

Especially since her hands worked faster than those of her *mamm*, and she was tucking the last of the strands into her prayer *kapp* while Clara was still working on the braids.

"I remember when I used to be able to braid

NEW YEAR'S PROMISE

like that," Clara commented. "But perhaps you should check on your *sohn* if you're done? He may want his *mamm*, and I don't think that your *daed* is prepared to be left alone with a crying *boppli* if it came down to it. He wasn't prepared when you and Noami were younger. Why would he be now?"

"That was exactly my thought, actually," Beth admitted. "Will you be all right with doing the braid on your own?"

"I'll be fine," she reassured Beth. "Go check on Eli and your *daed*. I'll be able to do something when I get the inspiration. Or just keep going slowly. Who knows?"

With that, Beth walked out of the room to find her *daed* and Eli. They were in the living room, just as they had been left. Her *daed* held Eli on his lap as they looked out the window at the snow falling to the ground. Beth hoped that the heavy snowfall might not prevent them from being able to go out to celebrate, knowing that they had experienced worse during previous winters.

"There you two are," Beth said. "How's he doing for you, *Daed*?"

"He's doing *wunderbar*, Beth," Amos said as he held Eli steady. "I don't think he wants to be anywhere else. He'll probably enjoy the ride to the King *haus*. Where's Clara?"

"Still finishing her braid," Beth replied. "I thought it would be a *gut* idea to *kumm* check on you two. She'll be done in a few minutes. Hopefully."

Her *daed* nodded.

It wasn't long before they were able to head to the King *haus*, as her *mamm* finished doing her hair shortly thereafter. Many others were already there, and she was not entirely surprised to find Samuel among the crowd together with Irene and Daniel who were playing with the other *kinner* who had accompanied their parents. He walked over to her with a large smile.

She walked with Eli in her arms. He wasn't quite stable enough on his little feet to maneuver amongst a crowd on his own. She didn't want to lose sight of him, either, so he would stay in her arms until the crowd had thinned sufficiently.

"I was starting to wonder when you would show up, Beth," Samuel teased her. "It is thanks to you, after all, that Leah was reinstated to the community. I believe she and her *familye* have much to thank you for."

Beth blushed as she put Eli down on the floor to crawl around near her feet.

"I only convinced the bishop that her spiritually questioning the traditions of our community showed a conviction that this community should be proud of, not shunning or pushing away," she clarified. "I suppose if that's as genuinely miraculous as people are calling it, then I am a miracle worker this week."

Samuel gave a hearty laugh.

"Well, I'm glad that you were able to *kumm*, regardless. I would have been sorry to miss you here," he said. "Would you like me to watch Eli so that you can relax? I'm sure your parents would also be remiss if they didn't get a break every now and then. Besides, Irene and Daniel are big enough now that I feel they can watch after themselves and each other and if they absolutely need me, they can find me." He offered her a smile.

She nodded slowly.

"That would be great, but there is such a crowd here that I am afraid that I wouldn't be able to relax unless I was able to see Eli," she replied. "I'm sorry if that's a bit of a dealbreaker for you."

Samuel shook his head.

"Not at all. I think the fact that you are caring so much for your *sohn* only shows that you have a lot of love to give," he said. "I wouldn't want to court anyone else, honestly."

Beth's blush grew deeper. They had talked about starting a courtship, but she hadn't thought he was entirely serious about it. Something about the fact that they were both widowed left a taste in her mouth that she couldn't quite identify, but she also knew that he was one of the few people in the community who could identify with the struggles of being a single parent.

If remaining a widower wasn't strength in a community that prized a full *familye* above all else, she didn't know where she could find a good example of it in the community.

"I didn't think you were serious about wanting to court me, Samuel," she finally admitted.

"Why wouldn't I be serious about it?" He raised an eyebrow, tilting his head to the side. "I have always been serious about who I court, and when it comes to who I want raising my *kinner* alongside me, I have devoted much thought to the qualities of the woman I would start courting when I felt ready to do so. Beth, you meet many of the qualifications I decided on, and I'd like to give a proper courtship a try. I realize it may not be quite enough time passing since your husband passed away for you to feel comfortable with it. However, if you are comfortable, I would be more than happy to at least see where a courtship leads."

Beth pressed her lips together. She had not imagined that she would end up in a courtship so soon after Jacob died. There was no recommended time within the community, but the current wisdom was that one could court again as soon as one felt ready. Some people took years to get there, and others didn't – but took years to feel as though it would be acceptable depending on who they had originally been married to.

"You don't even need to give me an answer tonight if you do not wish to," Samuel continued. "It is a big ask, and a big reply. When you have an answer, you can find me to give it."

"What kind of courtship would we have? What would it be built on?" Beth asked.

She thought this a *gut* place to start. If he wanted to court her, he had to give her proper answers. Besides, it never hurt to start with a good understanding of where they stood with each other. She had asked Jacob to do the same thing for her when they had first started their courtship.

"I'd like to have our courtship based on something simple: trust," he said. "I understand that it is what a courtship ought to be built on, but there is so much to go on that it deserves to be said properly."

Beth pursed her lips.

She had not thought that she would be interested in courtship so soon after Jacob had passed away. However, the time it took Samuel to answer her question was enough time for her to realize That this courtship wouldn't be rooted in trust alone. While it was a good foundation, this one would also be built on mutual care and understanding.

After at least a year of being single parents in the community together, where that was not the norm, she suspected that there was more to the way he felt about her than he was ready to admit right now. Perhaps even to himself. It all felt right, though.

"I think a courtship would be a lovely idea," she finally said. "But I'm not sure that I want to announce it to the rest of the community just yet."

He nodded slowly.

"Completely understandable, considering how quickly this would be happening after your husband's death," he said. "I'm sorry that it happened, but I am glad that it's given us this opportunity. Being a single parent here isn't the easiest option, and I'm sorry that you've had to do it so suddenly."

"I do appreciate that you had a warning," Beth said. "Having lost your *fraa* to illness couldn't have been easy, but neither was losing Jacob so suddenly and in such secrecy." She shook her head. "But I am very glad that the opportunity to find another place to belong has *kumm* out of the tragedy. We have nothing if we cannot find the best in our tragedies."

"Indeed," Samuel said.

CHAPTER 20

Soon after the new year, Naomi paced the hall of the bishop's home, anxiously awaiting the council's decision on the revised bakery annex plan. Because of the holidays, they had decided to come to a decision after a quick deliberation. They could have also been trying to avoid having to be accountable to Isaac, as he would have happily hunted down another answer if he needed to. That was part of Isaac's job in keeping the bakery running: if they were having to deal with the council, he was more likely to get the answer quickly and get it done properly.

For some reason, the council felt that they could wait to answer Naomi. Perhaps it was because they thought that the bakery still belonged to her parents. In a way, it did, but it was in the stages of being passed to Naomi now that she was ready to take it on. Beth had never wanted to be in charge, and this annex plan had fallen to Naomi and Isaac due to Eli, Beth's struggles, and her parents' wishes to be with their grandson instead of in the heat of the oven all day long every day of the week.

Isaac caught her hand as she passed him again, and she stopped her pacing. Even if only momentarily to see what he wanted.

"You're making me anxious watching you pace like this," he said. "Take a seat. They won't be delivering their answer any faster if they can hear you pacing around out here like a maniac, Naomi."

She pursed her lips. Isaac usually had a point, and she didn't want to make him feel as though she wasn't listening. But she didn't think that she could sit still right now. There was too much to worry about, and she wanted to know that she was going to get her answer. Sooner rather than later.

"I don't think I can physically sit still," she admitted to him. "The pacing is helping me focus on something other than the bakery annex and what the council is going to say. I know that we addressed their concerns in the revisions but knowing that they used the mistakes of my *rumspringa* in their reasoning for initially rejecting it, hurts. I worry that they'll find a way to make those relevant no matter what kind of revisions we do, and *Mamm* and *Daed* will be stuck having to make the annex plan."

Isaac chuckled softly, squeezing her hand as he did so.

"Then I suppose I have no reason to keep you from continuing to pace."

With that, he let go of her hand. She appreciated that and resumed her pacing. As she focused on her footsteps – one in front of the other and keeping her pace steady – she wondered what they were going to do if this revision was also rejected. A secondary rejection for an annex wasn't unheard of, but it was one of the rarest motions the council passed.

It usually took more work to convince the council to pass an annex if it had been rejected twice. With the amount of work that they had put into these revisions, Naomi wasn't sure that they had it in them to undertake the amount of work required to make sure that they were happy with the revisions if it was rejected again. She only wanted to be able to make sure that they were able to keep the bakery open. If they couldn't keep up with demand, customers were going to get fussier than they were right now.

If the customers got fussy, their ratings would almost certainly plummet. Perhaps that had been part of the council's plan, but she highly doubted it. They had been happy to see how much business the bakery was doing instead of watching it go out of business. Knowing that they had rejected the annex felt more as though they were worried the bakery would start doing too much business. As much as they wanted to keep the community peaceful and tranquil, there was only so much they could do if the bakery saw a marked increase in business from the *Englischer* sector.

Naomi only stopped her pacing when the door opened that separated the living room from the office room in which the council was deliberating. She turned to face the bishop, who had come to deliver the motion himself.

"Your annex plans for the bakery have been noted, and the revisions looked over," the bishop said. "The council agrees that you've successfully put together a plan that will keep the *Englischers* from disrupting the peace more than they already are. It's been approved."

Naomi let out a breath she hadn't even realized she was holding.

"That's *wunderbar* to hear!" Isaac smiled widely as he spoke. "What happened to change their minds? We heard there were other reasons they had originally decided to reject the annex."

"They were also worried about Naomi's past during her *rumspringa* influencing people's decision to support the bakery," the bishop revealed. "However, I reminded them that she has not been in contact with any of her friends from that time since she returned from her *rumspringa*. Besides, if I remember correctly, none of those friends were too happy about the fact that you were Amish."

Naomi nodded.

"They all thought I would be throwing my life away if I returned instead of continuing to party with them. The argument where I decided I had gone too far is burned in my memory," she shared. "I don't know why the council believes that is still a relevant part of my life. If I haven't brought it up and haven't shared more about that time of life with others, why is it considered a possible and viable threat to the peace of the community?"

"I don't entirely understand it, either, but I

was able to remind them of just what you've done for our community since returning and being baptized," the bishop shared. "You and your *familye* are among the most steadfast members of our community. I don't think that the council would discount that unless they were truly worried."

Naomi smiled a little. To hear that the bakery annex had been accepted was a great announcement, but to hear that she was finally overcoming the last of the challenges presented to her because of the way she had decided to live her *rumspringa* was even better.

"Well, I say this calls for celebration," Isaac said. "We've not only had the annex approved, but I believe Naomi has had some of her worst fears assuaged because of this conversation. Perhaps we should go tell your *familye* that the future is secured and that there will be no reason to despair for a while?"

She nodded.

"That would be a great way to end the day," she said. "I do believe my parents are at their *haus*. They may be watching Eli."

"Well, have a great night, then," the bishop said as he escorted them to the door. "I'm glad to hear that you are excited over what's happened here tonight. Please, make sure that you do business properly. I would hate to give the council a reason to regret approving your annex plans."

Naomi nodded slowly. There was really nothing more to say, so they walked out of the bishop's *haus* quietly. She held Isaac's hand for a moment, quietly reassuring herself that they were going to be all right. Then, she pulled her hand away. Isaac didn't seem to mind; in fact, it was almost as if he was letting her pull away when she was ready.

"Is Beth supposed to be out with Samuel?" Isaac asked once they were sure they were alone.

"I think she might be," Naomi admitted. "I don't know her schedule all that well since I no longer live at home, but I wouldn't be surprised to learn that they had offered to watch Eli, Irene, and Daniel to let them get a proper dinner or to just be alone."

"Well, I'm glad that she appears to be moving on quite well without any worry about who is watching her back," Isaac said. "She deserves a happy life. To have learned about Jacob's death as she did… it is a wonder that she's bounced back as quickly as she has to find happiness. I'm glad for her, don't get me wrong, but I hope that she is not doing this because she wants to return to a sense of normalcy more than anything else."

"Beth is not the kind of woman who would go out with a *mann* just to find a *daed* for her child." Naomi gave Isaac a stern look. "We are not *Englisch* women!"

This got a good chuckle out of Isaac, and Naomi found it hard to resist her own laughter. She had meant that statement as a bit of a chastisement for thinking that Beth would even consider only entering a courtship to find a father for her child. Isaac appeared to see the genius in her statement and not only agreed but found it funny!

"Well, for her sake, I hope you're right," Isaac said once the laughter had died down. "There would be nothing worse for her than feeling as though she has nothing more to do or say than be a *mamm* to her child. While motherhood is one of the greatest things a woman can achieve, it is not to be done alone. I cannot fathom how Samuel has done it all alone and held a job. Beth's been able to do it with the help of your parents… but he hasn't even had that kind of help to sustain him."

"I don't know how he did it before his younger one was of school age," Naomi said, "but I am glad that he's found a way to balance it all. I hope for their sake he is able to keep it up, no matter what happens between him and Beth."

With that, they had arrived at her parents' home. They walked inside to find her parents with Eli, as she had thought.

"What brings you two here so late?" Amos asked. "I knew Beth was going to be home late, so we're getting ready to put Eli to bed."

"We'll only be here a few minutes," Naomi clarified. "Can you spare a few minutes?"

EPILOGUE

Epiphany rolled around, and Naomi couldn't help but feel as though she had come to find the greatest joy in the world with her *familye* around her. On January sixth each year, the *familye* gathered to celebrate the happiness and the joy that had been found in the year before. It was supposed to bear good tidings for the year to come and help ring in the new year with feelings of happiness, luck, and other good emotions all around. Most celebrated on their own, but Naomi was glad that they were able to celebrate as a *familye* this year.

She sat down at the dining room table, beside Isaac. Beth had invited Samuel to celebrate with them this year, and it was quite a full room because of that. Inviting Samuel meant that Irene and Daniel came, too. There was absolutely nothing wrong with this; it simply meant the room was louder than Naomi was used to it being at this time of the year.

Sitting with Isaac to one side of her and Beth to the other, Naomi was afforded a chance to think about what had happened this year. After her and Isaac's wedding, she had been able to start working in the bakery full time because they needed to support a *haus* on it. Her parents had been gracious enough to let them live with them until their *haus* was built.

Eli had grown beautifully to be a year old. He was teetering around the room, testing out his balance and the feel of the wood under his feet. It was a glorious sight, being able to watch her nephew learn how to walk and crawl and grow as an individual. She wondered if her parents had always thought it had been a good sight, too.

"To a *gut year*," her *daed* said, quieting everyone down as he started the toast. "We have all had our struggles, but no year is without its challenges. We've had a great year finding our way around the challenges, and I'm sure there is plenty to come in the new year. I hope that we can use the happiness we have found along the way to get us through the new trials and that we will be able to overcome all that stands in our path."

There was a general set of cheers after this toast, and Naomi took a sip of her water once they were all done cheering her *daed* for a speech well made. Isaac turned to her with a smile once he had set his cup down.

"I'm sure that there will be plenty of reasons we struggle in the future but knowing that the bakery annex was accepted by the council is a weight off my shoulders. It was a lot of work," he said softly.

"I appreciate all the work you put into making sure the plan would meet their requirements. It's a weight off my shoulders as well." She smiled at him. "You're a *Wunderbar* man to do all of that without being asked. Is there anything I can do to show you how much it meant to me that you were willing to take on the challenge?"

"You don't have to do anything to show me how much you appreciate it," he said. "Just being here, talking to me... that's enough for me. I would do anything to make you happy, Naomi.

Even if it requires an explanation on my part, no matter how uncomfortable or how jealous it'll make you. I want our marriage to last, and that means there are no secrets."

"No secret sounds like a *gut* idea," she said. "Why didn't we do that before?"

Isaac laughed a little.

"It's in the spirit of learning and growing with the partner you've married, I suppose, not to know that there shouldn't be any secrets the first year," he mused. "But you're right. If we had known that this would be a better option, I believe we would have started with the no secrets pact."

Naomi nodded.

What mattered to her now wasn't that they had found a way to overcome the challenges brought about by the letters – though that obviously mattered to her – but that she had been reminded of something she easily forgot somehow. *Gott* was always with her, even in her darkest moments. That was enough for her to remember that there was plenty to do when the world seemed like it was falling apart.

Isaac took her hand and squeezed it carefully.

"I love you, Naomi," he said softly. "No matter what happens, I want you to remember that. I love you too much to give that life up without doing whatever is needed. And that much will remain true, no matter what challenges the coming year might bring."

"I'm glad to know all of that."

She squeezed his hand in response. Everyone was too focused on the meal to pay them any attention, which made her feel much better about being a little more open with their intimacy. She dared to press a kiss to his cheek, which made him blush.

∼

AFTER HER *DAED* GAVE the toast, Beth couldn't focus on anyone but Samuel. He had slipped away to check on Irene, but he had raised his water cup in a toast with them as they had rung in the new year. She wasn't mad that he had gone to check on his *dochder*. What kind of *daed* would he be if he didn't at least check on his *kinner* when they called for him? It could have been an issue of the sort that required him to leave immediately, and it could have been a scraped knee at her age.

It was always better to at least check on Irene and Daniel.

When he returned, he turned to her.

"I think your *daed's* toast to the new year was quite well put together," he said. "I don't think I could have said it better myself. Besides, to ring in the new year with a *familye* this year instead of just my *kinner* feels *gut*. My parents not being in this community makes it so difficult sometimes…"

"Why did you not return to their community when your *fraa* died? If I understand it correctly, she was the reason you moved here," Beth said. "I understand if you do not wish to talk about it, but I must confess that this question has been nagging at the back of my mind for quite some time."

"It's all right," Samuel said. "I've had many ask that question, but not all of them have the best intentions behind asking it. You, I can tell, wish only to know so that you can see what has happened. Well, in all honesty, I was not incredibly attracted to any of the women in my community. When I met my late *fraa* on her *rumspringa*, I was struck by her beauty and her grace. I knew I wanted to live out the rest of my days in the community in which she had grown up."

"And you committed to doing just that when your *fraa* passed?" Beth asked, raising an eyebrow.

He nodded slowly.

"And my parents never quite forgave me for deciding to leave for a kinder community. I grew up in a community much stricter than this, though I suppose that you find this community quite strict," he continued. "I vowed that my parents would never be able to teach my *kinner* to fear them as I feared them growing up. If you wish to raise Eli with rules that are not as strict, I will adjust my rules to help you do that. Strictness can always be eased."

"Is that part of why you've clashed with the elders so often while raising your *kinner*?"

"They know I was raised in a stricter community and find it odd that I am only adhering to the tenants that are taught here instead of leaving to raise my *kinner* where I grew up," he admitted. "And I worry that sometimes, they hold it against me. But I wouldn't take my *kinner* away from what they know."

Beth nodded slowly.

This conversation had taken a direction she hadn't predicted, but that was all right with her. She had wanted to learn more about Samuel to start the new year right, and she was glad she had asked the biggest question looming in the back of her mind. Knowing that he wouldn't get the same kind of support in his community as he got here answered so many questions.

It also allowed her to go forward with this courtship with an eye towards marriage. She had not originally thought that she would already be thinking about marriage just a year after Jacob's death. Samuel had a different kind of demeanor about him. He wasn't afraid to be wrong in the eyes of the community to raise his *kinner* as he felt they needed to be raised.

That was the same kind of parenting she wished to use to raise Eli. She simply hadn't found the confidence to do it on her own. Perhaps married to Samuel, she would find the confidence to stand up for the way they were raising their *kinner*.

She glanced at Naomi and Isaac, chatting away in a corner. Perhaps about what the new year would bring, and perhaps about whatever had been going on between the two of them. She knew that Isaac had been worried about Naomi since pulling her out of the frozen lake.

"Beth, I know it is a little soon to start talking marriage, as far as our courtship goes," Samuel said, pulling her out of her thoughts. "However, I want you to know that I would not have started this courtship if I did not mean to follow through. That said, we need not follow through on the intentions of a courtship until you feel ready to share your life and your heart with me. Just by courting, we are sharing with the community that we mean to marry someday."

Beth smiled a little.

"Marriage is not yet on my mind, but I'll admit that the thought has crossed my mind once or twice since we started. Perhaps later in the year, it'll be a thought to entertain."

Samuel smiled broadly, and without a word, took her hand and stared at her, his eyes sparkling. Beth felt a gentle warmth come over her, and she smiled back before getting up to tend to her little Eli.

∼

Click here to get notification when the next book is available, and to hear about other good things I give my readers (or copy and paste this link into your browser: *bit.ly/Grace-FreeBook*).
You will also receive a free copy of *Rumspringa's Promise, Secret Love* **and** *River*

Blessings**, exclusive spinoffs from the *Seasons of Love*, *Amish Hearts* and the *Amish Sisters series*** for members of my Readers' Group. These stories are NOT available anywhere else.

FREE DOWNLOAD

EXCLUSIVE and FREE for subscribers of my Readers' Group

CLICK HERE!

(or copy and paste this link into your browser: *bit.ly/Grace-FreeBook*)

NOTE FROM THE AUTHOR

Thank you for taking a chance on *New Year's Promise,* Book 2 of the *Tales of Amish Sisters* series.

Did you enjoy the book? I hope so, and I would really appreciate it if you would help others enjoy this book, and help spread the word.

Please consider leaving a review today telling other readers why you liked this book, wherever you purchased this book, or on Goodreads. **It doesn't need to be long**, just a few sentences can make a huge difference. **Your reviews go a long way in helping others discover what I am writing**, and decide if a book is for them.

I appreciate anything you can do to help, and if you do write a review, wherever it is, please send an email at grace@gracelewisauthor.com, so I could thank you personally.

Here are some places where you can leave a review:

- Amazon.com;
- Goodreads.

Thank you for reading, and have a lovely day,

Grace Lewis

PS: I love hearing from my readers. Feel free to email me directly at grace@gracelewisauthor.com (or to connect with me on Facebook here https://www.facebook.com/GraceLewisAuthor). I read and respond to every message.

EXCLUSIVE CHRISTMAS BOXSET: 15 TALES OF LOVE, FAMILY AND CHRISTMAS CELEBRATION

Dear Readers,

For a limited time this Christmas (extended to January 2024), we are delighted to offer a special boxset that contains not only the first 15 books of our beloved series but also includes the 4 first books of **Amish Christmas Blessings** series. It's a treasure trove of stories that will fill your holidays with the spirit of Amish romance and the magic of Christmas.

>> **Copy and paste this link: amazon.com/dp/B0CKQBF7R4** into your browser to get this special 15 books Boxset.

GRACE LEWIS

Don't miss this chance to own this special collection. It's the perfect way to cozy up and enjoy the holiday season, wrapped in the tender and inspiring tales of our Amish community.

>> **Copy and paste this link: amazon.com/dp/B0CKQBF7R4** into your browser to get this special 15 books Boxset.

Warm wishes and happy reading,

Grace Lewis

OTHER BOOKS BY GRACE LEWIS

꧁꧂

Click here to browse all Grace Lewis's Books (or copy and paste this link into your browser: *bit.ly/gracelewisauthor*).

CHRISTMAS AWAKENING – AMISH CHRISTMAS BLESSINGS SERIES, BOOK 5 (EXCERPT)

Christmas Awakening Summary

In the season of giving, will Mary's longing to teach disrupt the Yuletide peace in her family?

In the quaint Amish town of Dalton in Kingston, the Yuletide season brings more than just snowflakes and sleigh bells for Mary and Moses Lapp. Amidst the twinkling Christmas lights and the scent of fresh pine, Mary Lapp, blessed with three beautiful children and a loving husband, finds herself grappling with a longing for something more. As the festive spirit envelops the town, her heart yearns to return to her passion for teaching, reigniting a spark that once brought her immense joy.

But as the snow blankets the peaceful streets, resistance comes from the most unexpected place – her own home. Moses Lapp, her devoted husband, basks in the contentment of their thriving farm and the warmth of their family life. Unseen challenges begin to encroach upon his idyllic world. Clinging to faith and love, Moses is determined to face these trials head-on, yet he remains blind to the growing restlessness in his wife.

Their once harmonious home now echoes with the silent tension of unspoken dreams and unmet desires. Mary's resolve to teach clashes with Moses' wish for her to remain the heart of their home. As Christmas approaches, their disagreement casts a shadow over the festive preparations, and even their children sense the growing divide.

In this heartwarming tale set against the backdrop of an Amish Christmas, Mary and Moses must navigate the delicate balance between personal aspirations and familial responsibilities. Will the magic of the season guide them back to each other, or will their differences push them further apart? Can they find a way to blend Mary's dreams with the needs of their family, rekindling not just the spirit of Christmas but the flame of their love?

Unwrap the gift of love, understanding, and new beginnings in this captivating Amish romance, where the true meaning of Christmas shines through the struggles and joys of Mary and Moses Lapp.

>> **copy and paste this link into your browser:** *bit.ly/Grace-FreeBook* to be notified when the book is available.

CHAPTER ONE

Mary sat on her porch early in the morning, a shawl wrapped around her shoulders. It had snowed the night before, leaving the world white and perfectly ready for the coming Christmas season. It was not the snow that had her on the porch this morning. That honor went to her *kinner*: her eight-year-old twins, Faith and Elijah, and her beautiful young *dochder* Ruth who had come to their *familye* six years ago.

This was the first snow of the year, and it had come down gently. There couldn't have been more than a few inches of snow, which left plenty of space for her *kinner* to jump in the leaves that Moses had raked up yesterday.

Sitting on the porch with her, Addie held up a sample of crochet work. In the last few years,

Mary had become rather good at crocheting. Despite her initial feelings about the craft, she had to admit that she liked it. She looked up when she heard loud giggles, louder than she would have expected from the *kinner* as they jumped around in the leaves.

She looked up to see the twins getting ready to throw their younger *schweschder* into the pile of leaves, which would have certainly scattered the leaves everywhere.

"You know," Mary said softly as she put her crochet sample in her lap to look up at the three of them, "if you make such a mess, you'll have to clean it up. And the snow has made it that much harder to clean up leaves today. Are you sure that you want to make a mess of these leaves?"

The three *kinner* looked at each other, then at Mary, and then all shook their heads.

"That's what I thought. Perhaps it's time for you three to come inside and get warm again before you continue," she said.

The *kinner* frowned.

"But *Mamm!*" Faith whined. "We're having fun."

"Then be careful you don't get too cold," Mary said softly. "I don't want to see any of you get hurt either. Do you understand me?"

They all nodded.

With that, Mary returned her attention to the crochet work in her lap for but a moment.

The front door opened behind her, which meant that Moses was ready to leave for a day of work in his carpentry shop. That carpentry shop had been the reason that they had been able to afford what they needed, and she appreciated all the work that went into what he did. It was hard, strenuous labor, and he did it without a care in the world.

"I'll see you when I get home," Moses said before pressing a soft kiss to Mary's forehead. "Oh… that's a beautiful piece of crochet, dear. I cannot believe how *gut* you've gotten. I marvel at it." He gave her a smile, which only caused her to blush a little bit.

"*Danke.* See you when you get home, Moses," Mary said with a smile.

Faith, Elijah, and Ruth each hugged him on his way out of the yard, which Mary found an endearing sight. They were all clinging to his waist, with his arms around them as best as he could get them. Eventually, he sent them back to the yard, and off Moses walked towards his carpentry shop. He'd taken to walking there in the mornings and home in the evenings when it snowed to save the horse the trouble and to avoid it slipping on the ice and snow that had already melted and refrozen.

The *kinner* returned to playing in the leaves and snow, which was fine by Mary. She didn't get to enjoy a lot of time with Addie since having the *kinner* and Addie had never much been one to yearn for that milestone in her life.

Once Moses was out of sight, she turned to Addie with a soft sigh.

"Would you believe that I miss going to work every morning and feeling useful?" she said, shaking her head, "I love my *kinner*, and I wouldn't trade them for anything in the world, but they're at that age where I could get a job out of the *haus* during the school year and they wouldn't know the difference. Especially Ruth now."

"Well, I know that I may not have the best advice," Addie cautioned. "I don't entirely understand that feeling having worked my entire life and never married. However, if that's truly how you feel, why don't you apply for the new teaching position at the school? They only have Edna Troyer in the school now. Elise left for Pennsylvania to marry that *mann* she met while you were pregnant with the twins and hasn't returned since. They're struggling to fill the spot."

Mary pursed her lips.

"I suppose that is an option," she said. "I'm not sure that I could return to teaching considering that there are usually only unmarried women in those positions. But if the position needs to be filled desperately, there's no harm in trying."

"Especially since that is what most people will remember you for," Addie piped up. "That's where you got your start when Moses courted you, and I think that there are plenty of people who are getting ready to leave the school who fondly remember the years you taught."

"I'll have to look into it and see what I can do," Mary said, her voice lighter than it had been when wishing Moses a happy day at the carpentry shop. "But for now, what do you think of this piece? Moses said it was beautiful when he left, but… I don't know what I think of it. I spent a lot of time getting the stitches to work properly, but it still appears to be lopsided."

Addie laughed a little.

"That's what it is supposed to look like, Mary," Addie said. "It's not the easiest thing in the world, but you're right, it's far too lopsided. People would be able to tell immediately that you're learning if you wanted to put it into a larger piece."

Mary sighed.

"I suppose there's really nothing I can do about that unless I practice more," she said. "I crochet when the *kinner* take naps, but that's really the only chance I have to do it nowadays. When they were younger, I could crochet all day long unless they were feeding, because they slept a lot."

"And now it feels like they have far too much energy?" Addie raised an eyebrow.

"*Nee*, but there have been days I've wondered if I ended up taking them into the city by accident – knowing that there was no way I could have done that accidentally," Mary admitted. "They remind me of how I used to act as a *kind*, and I'm so sorry for my parents now. I wonder if Moses has the same thoughts or if he's been able to escape that kind of thinking."

"He may not escape all of it, but that doesn't mean he doesn't agree," Addie said. "Have you talked to Moses about your wish to have a job again? To feel useful?"

Mary wasn't entirely surprised the conversation returned to the topic of her feeling useless at home with the *kinner* since Ruth was the only *kind* at home during the school year and that would be changing come the start of the new school year.

"He was the one who suggested I take up crocheting, actually," Mary admitted. "He saw how much I wanted to do something with my hands, and we both knew I didn't have time to garden when the twins were younger. So, one day he surprised me with some beginner patterns, some yarn, and a few crochet hooks, just because he could. Said he thought this would be helpful and I could learn to crochet for our *kinner*."

"So that's where they all got those quilts that they talk about so proudly," Addie mused. "We've all wondered how they could have crocheted pieces of the quilts, too. You did that when they were young, didn't you?"

"I did. It was something that I could do while they were asleep without worrying too much about waking them up," she said, shrugging. "That was always the largest worry: waking them up when I was doing something while they slept. And I couldn't exactly leave the *haus* in case they woke up unless I wanted to have a sleeping *boppli* or two with me."

"Well, I know one thing from all the time we've talked between when you first arrived in

Dalton and now," Addie started, "and that is that you'll find something to keep you occupied. You always do."

Mary smiled.

"Well, for now, that's talking about crochet with you while we watch the *kinner* in the snow so that they don't make an utter mess of the yard, specifically that pile of leaves they've been jumping into all morning. I'm surprised no one has complained about hitting a stick yet with their knee, or their face. I don't want that to happen, but it's a leaf pile."

Addie nodded with a soft chuckle.

"Well, whatever the outcome of this morning's playtime is," she said, "I know that you'll be there to comfort them if something *does* go wrong. You've always been a *Wunderbar mamm*, Mary. I'm sure that you'll find something that will allow you to work and still take care of the *familye*."

Mary smiled at her friend.

"I think I needed to hear that from you. *Danke*," Mary said. "Now… what about your crochet? What have you been doing lately?"

Addie smiled and produced her crochet sample. It was made in white yarn, which she thought was rather adventurous. Usually, they attempted to crochet pieces that would match, color-wise, with the rest of their wardrobes.

"I've taken up some bridal crochet on the side," she admitted. "*English* brides will pay very well for crocheted flowers for their bouquets. I'm working on a calla lily right now. A white one, of course, and then some blue ones for the rest of the wedding party. At least, that's what the customer said. I have a lot of free time when no one's staying in the boarding *haus*. I don't charge much, but they appreciate my honesty about timing. The wedding this one is for is about a year away."

"I remember always thinking I'd do fake flowers at my wedding, before marrying Moses, anyway," Mary said. "Crocheted flowers would be such a beautiful keepsake for the wedding party, too, since they can be displayed like regular silk flowers without much worry about the fabric crinkling."

Addie smiled.

"I decided I'd do the bride's bouquet first because I love white calla lilies," she said. "The blue ones she wants are a little odd, but I suppose it makes sense if that's going to be the color scheme she wants. Then again, that's probably why she wanted fake flowers in the first place."

Mary nodded.

They finished their conversation a moment later because Ruth came running up to the porch crying about having fallen on a branch, exactly as Mary predicted someone might a few minutes ago.

"Well, I do believe that is my cue to go for the day," Addie joked. "I'll see you around, Mary. Will you be all right?"

"*Jah*. I can handle this," Mary said. "*Danke* for listening."

With that, Addie gave the *kinner* hugs and made her way back to the lodging *haus*. As Addie disappeared into the distance, Mary took the *kinner* inside to warm up by the fireplace and to treat Ruth's injured knee.

Though she loved all three of them, Mary couldn't exactly lie to herself and say she was not thrilled about the idea of applying for the teaching position. Addie knew her far too well.

>> copy and paste this link into your browser: *bit.ly/Grace-FreeBook* **to be notified when the book is available.**

THE SEASONS OF LOVE SERIES

The Seasons of Love series follows the journey of seven siblings in an Amish community as they navigate their desires and dreams in life, which lead them to complicated relationships with each other and potential suitors. The series shows the unbreakable bond between the Mast siblings as they face the ups and downs of their romantic lives.

Each book is a stand-alone read, but to make the most of the series you should consider reading them in order.

>> Copy and paste this link: amazon.com/dp/B0BZ5BDK5Q into your browser to read it now.

What readers are saying about the Seasons of Love series:

Book 1: Spring of Virtue

★★★★★ Grace Lewis did a wonderful job of writing this book. The characters had interesting personalities, the story line was different, and the outcome was endearing. I definitely recommend this book.

★★★★★ I loved the entire book. I didn't want to put it down. The characters came to life as I read the story.

Book 2: Summer of Longing

★★★★★ I am really enjoying this series. Each story is very well written and each of them are different. I look forward to reading all of them.

★★★★★ **An Endearing Story, for sure!** I loved the main characters from the very beginning. I loved the way the story unfolded right before your eyes. Definitely a book to be recommended. The author wrote a truly lovely and welcoming story. Thank you.

Book 3: Indian Summer Turmoil

★★★★★ Indian Summer Turmoil is such a

delightful read. I love the characters and their real dilemmas. Trying to live out your life and make others happy is a burden God doesn't mean for us to carry. The Twists and turns are real and true love wins. Which makes a great read!

Book 4: Harvesting Hope

⭐⭐⭐⭐⭐ What a delicious read this was! I love the sweetness and the real emotional conflict of parents and daughter. You don't want to miss this one, for sure.

Book 5: Winter's Whisper

⭐⭐⭐⭐⭐ **The series is fantastic!** Every book turned out to be beautiful and fascinating. I truly went from one book to the next with passion to find out more.

⭐⭐⭐⭐⭐ **Wonderful!** This book was another can't put down until reading every word. I was so happy when Joanne decided to not marry the old man her Father's age. Sometimes patience is the name of the game. Year's ago, I had to learn to be patient, never thinking it would be that many year's.

Book 6: Blossoming into Family

⭐⭐⭐⭐⭐ **Great series!** I thoroughly enjoyed

every single book in this series! Each story was different, with a great lesson as well. Sometimes I do not like series books, but this one I thoroughly enjoyed.

⭐⭐⭐⭐⭐ A very sweet short story of how great it is to feel like you are accepted, cared for and loved. How great it is to have a close family.

>> Copy and paste this link: amazon.com/dp/B0BZ5BDK5Q into your browser to read it now.

This book is a work of fiction. Names, characters and places are either products of the author's imagination or used fictitiously. Any resemblance to actual persons, living or dead, events, locales or Amish communities is entirely coincidental. The author has taken liberties with locales, including the creation of fictional towns and places, as a mean of creating the necessary circumstances for the story. This books is intended for fictional purposes only, it is not a handbook on the Amish.

Copyright © 2024 by Grace Lewis

All rights reserved. Without limiting the rights under copyright reserved above, no part of this publication may be reproduced, stored in or introduced into a retrieval system, or transmitted in any form, or by any means (electronic, mechanical, photocopying, recording, or otherwise), without the prior written permission of the copyright owner, except for the use of brief quotations in a book review.

Made in the USA
Columbia, SC
07 March 2024